SENSUAL SURRENDER

THE SERAFINA: SIN CITY SERIES

Katie Reus

Sensual Surrender by Katie Reus Copyright © 2014
First Surrender by Katie Reus Copyright © 2013

All rights reserved. Except as permitted under the U.S. Copyright Act of 1976, no part of this publication may be reproduced, distributed, or transmitted in any form or by any means, or stored in a database or retrieval system, without the prior written permission of the author.

Cover art: Jaycee of Sweet 'N Spicy Designs

Publisher's Note: This is a work of fiction. Names, characters, places, and incidents are either the products of the author's imagination or used fictitiously, and any resemblance to actual persons, living or dead, or business establishments, organizations or locales is completely coincidental.

Sensual Surrender/Katie Reus. -- 1st ed.
ISBN-13: 978-1494811525
ISBN-10: 1494811529

For Kari Walker, who fell in love with Jay long before I wrote his story. I say this so often, but thank you again for always being in my corner. I couldn't ask for a better friend.

Praise for the novels of Katie Reus

"…an engrossing page-turner that I enjoyed in one sitting. Reus offers all the ingredients I love in a paranormal romance." —Book Lovers, Inc.

"Has all the right ingredients: a hot couple, evil villains, and a killer action-filled plot. . . . [The] Moon Shifter series is what I call Grade-A entertainment!" —Joyfully Reviewed

"I could not put this book down. . . . Let me be clear that I am not saying that this was a good book *for* a paranormal genre; it was an excellent romance read, *period.*" —All About Romance

"Reus strikes just the right balance of steamy sexual tension and nail-biting action.…This romantic thriller reliably hits every note that fans of the genre will expect." —*Publisher's Weekly*

"Prepare yourself for the start of a great new series! . . . I'm excited about reading more about this great group of characters." —Fresh Fiction

"Nonstop action, a solid plot, good pacing and riveting suspense…" —*RT Book Reviews (4.5 Stars)*

First Surrender
Copyright © 2013 by Katie Reus

CHAPTER ONE

Sierra took a subtle sniff of her upper arm as she rode the elevator up to the fiftieth floor of the new Serafina hotel and casino—owned by billionaire Wyatt Christiansen. As head chef at Cloud 9, one of the restaurants at the Serafina, she sometimes smelled like food at the end of a long shift even though she'd changed clothes. Okay, she always smelled like food. Which wasn't necessarily a bad thing, but she'd cooked a lot of seafood today. She didn't scent anything too strong but was sure her friend Hayden would tell her when she saw him. At least she'd changed out of her work clothes and chef's coat so she was comfortable in jeans and a fitted T-shirt.

He'd started work at the Serafina the same time she had. It had officially opened a year ago. She'd been brought over from one of Christiansen's other hotels to work here and Hayden had been hired after retiring from the Navy. Christiansen's wife Iris ran all the security at the hotel, but Hayden was directly under her as her second-in-command. Sierra didn't know how they handled the stress of security at such a mammoth hotel. She'd go cross-eyed trying to watch all those cameras at once. But, they had a good team with minimum problems.

As the elevator dinged, announcing her arrival to the security floor, damn butterflies took flight in her stomach. It always happened when she was about to see Hayden and she hated it. When she'd first met him, she thought he was a big jerk. A big, scary jerk. Okay, a sexy-as-hell jerk with tattooed sleeves covering both his arms. His tats added to that whole tall, dark and intimidating thing he had going on. As a former SEAL, Hayden certainly had the training for his current profession. But she'd come to learn that he was one of the sweetest men she'd ever known. For the last year they'd hung out constantly as friends and Thursday nights they had a standing ritual of dinner, drinks and sometimes she coerced him into going dancing with her and her friends. Usually he just stood guard by one of their tables and growled at any males who got too close. Which made her adore him even more.

God, she really was a masochist. Hayden was never going to be interested in her romantically but that didn't stop her from wanting him more and more every day. Hayden could have any woman he wanted and she knew she didn't fit the mold of his type. It was her freaking curse in life. Growing up and in college she had a lot of male friends because of her 'friendly' personality but she never dated any of them. One of her college friends had told her that she was way too 'the girl next door type', the type of girl you brought home to your mother—which was freaking annoying. She wanted to be the type of girl who got a man's pulse pounding out of control. The kind who got him so hot and bothered that he couldn't think straight. But not just any man. Only Hayden.

Her flat sandals snapped softly against the marble as she entered the security floor. A giant glass wall greeted her. Behind it she could see desks, and too many television screens to count. Some huge, some small, focused on dealers' hands, patrons, the various bars and pretty much anywhere legal a camera could go. The array of them still astounded her. Stopping at one of the glass doors, she placed her hand on the biometric scanner. Once it scanned her palm, the door immediately opened with a whoosh. She had no business up here but about eight months ago Hayden had programmed her into the system so she wouldn't have to bug him every Thursday. Sometimes she got off earlier than him and preferred to wait in the security room as opposed to the bar in her restaurant. She was there enough during the week; she didn't want to hang out in her off time too.

Stepping inside she was inundated with noise and frantic chatter. Men and women were talking into their headsets, some clearly worried. There was normally a fast pace up here but today it seemed different.

Glancing around, Sierra didn't see Hayden anywhere but assumed he was in his office. Before she'd taken two steps in that direction, Marty, one of the tech guys, jumped up from his desk when he saw her. "Hey, honey. What are you doing up here?"

She normally didn't like nicknames but Marty called every female honey. She smiled. "Just stopping by to see if Hayden could sneak away early."

Marty's eyes widened slightly. "Oh…he's not here. He said something about a date."

A date? The word was like a punch to her gut. For a moment she was totally stunned, but she wasn't going to show it in front of anyone, especially not a coworker. This place was worse than a middle school when it came to gossip. So she pasted on a smile. "Oh, right. He mentioned that, I totally forgot."

Marty started to respond but Iris Christiansen strode through the glass doorway looking fierce in black pants, a crisp white button down shirt and a sleek, clearly custom-made black jacket. Everything about the other woman was, well, fierce. She was gorgeous but also a little scary, especially since Sierra knew the former Marine was always well-armed. The tall woman gave Marty one look and he scampered away.

Luckily she gave Sierra a bright smile. "What's up, Sierra? You got a problem at the restaurant?"

Still struggling to find her voice, she shook her head. "No problem, just leaving. See you tomorrow." Sierra tried to hurry away, but Iris followed her to the elevators.

"What's going on? You don't look okay."

Sierra swallowed hard. Lord, was she that transparent? "Just had a long day. Busy, you know?" *Gah, why wouldn't the elevator hurry up?*

Iris raised a dark eyebrow. "Do I need to kick his ass?"

Staring at her, Sierra frowned. "What? Who?"

"Hayden. What's he done now?"

The mention of his name made Sierra's stomach flip-flop. It also pissed her off. If he'd had a date he could have had the decency to tell her. Shrugging jerkily, she breathed out a sigh of relief when the elevator stopped and dinged. "Hayden hasn't done anything." And she wondered why Iris would assume this had anything to do with the man. It wasn't like they were dating.

Iris didn't respond, but her lips pulled into a thin line as the doors shut behind Sierra. Once she was alone, Sierra didn't bother to keep up a happy face. Hayden hadn't mentioned dating anyone in the past year, though she knew the man had to be dating. He was walking, talking sex appeal. Absently she rubbed the center of her chest. So, he was dating. No big deal. Right? Ugh, yeah right. Swallowing back the traitorous tears threatening to overwhelm her, she hurried into the below ground parking garage. Normally Hayden or someone else walked her to her vehicle but she didn't want to bother asking anyone else. Not when she felt like crying. No way was she embarrassing herself and becoming a source of casino gossip.

Picking up her pace, her sandals slapped quickly across the concrete. As she reached the second row of cars, a tiny scream escaped her lips as a man wearing a mask jumped out from behind her Jeep. The guy was huge, maybe six feet tall, and when she saw the flash of metal—a knife!—in his hands, her chest constricted as a hundred horrible scenarios raced through her mind. Knowing she'd only get one chance she let out a blood-curdling scream at the top of her lungs as she back-tracked and started running in the other direction.

Blood rushed in her ears as she continued screaming and digging in her purse for her pepper spray. She knew she wouldn't be a physical match against anyone and—pain exploded in her scalp as he grabbed her by the hair and jerked back.

Instinctively she reached back to try to stop him and quickly realized her mistake. Using a lot of force, he slammed her forehead against a nearby car. Another burst of pain launched inside her skull as she tried to shove away from the vehicle. He pulled her head back again and she struggled to find breath—suddenly she was falling.

"Hey! Stop!" An angry male voice ricocheted off the walls of the parking garage and she heard multiple sets of footsteps pounding against the pavement as her palms hit the ground.

Rolling over, she raised her hands instinctively to fight off another blow but found Jay, Hayden's brother, racing toward her. It was hard to see because of the tears blurring her vision but he was hard to miss.

She struggled to stand but stopped and just sagged against the vehicle, thankful someone had been there to scare off her attacker. The side of her head ached but she didn't even care. Closing her eyes, she let her head fall back against the vehicle and didn't bother to fight the tears that poured out. When she thought about what could have happened...a sob wracked her body as she wrapped her arms around herself.

CHAPTER TWO

"*Come on*," Hayden muttered to his computer screen as it powered down. He wanted to get the fuck out of here and meet up with Sierra. Glancing at his cell, he frowned when he saw the time and started to text her. Normally he didn't bother her during working hours because she was just as busy as him and could barely look at her phone, but she should be off by now. As he started punching in letters, the glass door to his office opened.

Iris, his direct boss, stepped in looking pissed. At him. His eyebrows raised. He'd seen Iris angry at a lot of people, namely jackasses who'd tried to rob the place, but her ire had never been aimed at him. Before he could ask what was going on, she turned and snapped the shades down on the window to his office. It overlooked part of the security area, giving everyone open access to him and vice versa.

After giving them privacy, she dropped into one of the chairs in front of his desk. "What's going on with Sierra?"

That stopped him cold. Had something happened? Ice chilled his veins. "What do you mean?"

Iris's dark eyes narrowed accusingly. "I just saw her leaving and she looked upset. She tried to cover it, but she wears her emotions right out in the open. I swear if you hurt that girl—"

Hayden held up his hands. "What the hell, Iris? I'd *never* hurt Sierra." He'd rather cut off his own arm than cause her pain.

Iris immediately relaxed. "Okay, I figured you didn't do anything but had to be sure. We can't afford to lose her—I'd kill you for that alone. That woman can freaking cook."

Hayden rolled his eyes. Iris ate at Sierra's restaurant at least once a day, and he didn't know where the slim woman put it all. That wasn't what he cared about though. "So wait, Sierra was *here* and left?" They had a standing 'date' every Thursday night. It was his favorite night of the week even if it wasn't a real date. He wished it was though. The kind where she ended up back at his place, naked and underneath him as he pumped into her for hours. He needed to get over his bullshit and just make a move. It was hard though, because if he read her wrong and she rejected him—that thought pierced him in a way he couldn't even think about.

Iris nodded, her expression curious as she watched him.

Ignoring her for the moment, he picked up his phone and started to call Sierra when it rang. It was his brother. He picked up on the first ring. "Hey."

"I'm in parking garage B, section 210. Get your ass down here. Sierra's been hurt," Jay said hurriedly.

The words were like a punch to his system. Hayden jumped up and motioned for Iris to follow. Time seemed to slow down and everything around him sharpened into focus as they hurried toward the elevators. "How bad? What happened?" The thought of anything happening to Sierra...fuck, he couldn't even go there. Before he heard all the facts he needed to keep a level head.

"Someone attacked her, slammed her head against a car. She's got some bruising and she's upset but otherwise physically unharmed. The fucker got away because I had to check on her first. By the time I went after him there was no trace of him. The paramedics and police are on their way but I've got someone...hold on..." In the background he could hear Jay murmuring something then he was back on the line. "Listen, if you see Iris—"

"She's with me," he said as they stepped into the elevator. "We'll be there in less than a minute."

"Good."

As they disconnected, Hayden shoved his phone in his pants pocket. He quickly relayed what his brother had told him as the elevator started moving. He slid his master key into the panel so they would go directly to the parking garage. The ride was fast but it seemed like the longest minute of his entire life. As a former SEAL, he'd been on a shitload of brutal missions in war-torn countries, been stuck behind enemy lines with no backup for days, but nothing compared to the fear pumping through his veins now. Not only was Sierra the sweetest, most sensual woman he knew, she fucking owned him. Even if she didn't know it yet.

"Your brother said she's unhurt," Iris murmured, her voice unusually soft.

Hayden couldn't even respond. His vocal cords refused to work. After what felt like an eternity, the door finally opened and he raced out. Half a dozen men in security uniforms were standing guard, giving Sierra and Jay a ten foot radius. Hayden was sure his brother or someone had already started the hunt for whoever had tried to hurt her. Normally he'd take over the situation, but all he cared about was making sure Sierra was safe. He would deal with hunting down and destroying whoever had attacked her later.

CHAPTER THREE

Sierra's eyes widened when she saw Hayden barreling down on her and Jay. Her head throbbed, but Jay had gotten an ice pack for her which helped. Now they were waiting on the police so she could fill out a report. She'd have to make an official one at the casino too, but none of that concerned her now.

The craziest sense of relief pumped through her now that Hayden was here. She was still hurt that he'd apparently been going on some date, but she was grateful for his presence. At six feet five he was a freaking giant compared to her. Something she teased him about occasionally. Normally he wore a suit and tie to work but at the moment he just had on dark slacks and a buttoned up white shirt. His sleeves were rolled up, showing off his tattooed, incredibly muscular arms. Everything about him was big, intimidating and sexy.

Ignoring his brother, Hayden didn't stop until he was right in front of her, completely crowding her personal space. Even though she was standing, he had to bend down because of her shorter height. He cupped the left side of her head, gently rubbing his thumb over her cheek as he turned her head to look at the damage on the right side. She was too stunned by his touch to even think about protesting. Words caught in her throat as he lifted the ice pack away and made a low, menacing sound in his throat.

After a moment he turned her back so that she had to look directly at him. There were so many emotions in his gaze and he was still rubbing her cheek in a soft, sensual way that made all her pain fade. He'd never touched her like this before. Sure, they'd hugged and he occasionally slung an arm around her shoulders in a friendly way but this felt different somehow. Either that or she'd hit her head harder than she thought. It was probably the head thing.

"How're you feeling, baby?" he rasped out.

She blinked in shock. *Baby?* Her mouth partially opened as he leaned closer. For a moment she thought he was going to kiss her, but then she realized he was looking at her eyes. Of course he was. She felt like an idiot for thinking otherwise. He was trying to check if she had a concussion.

"Are you nauseated?" he asked quietly.

The concern she saw in his face was almost enough to make her burst into tears. She was trying to keep it together but with him there it was damn hard. "No."

"Did you lose consciousness?"

Jay had already asked her these questions but she just shook her head. "No."

"Are you feeling dizzy or tired? Do you hear a ringing in your ears?"

"No to all of the above."

"What about a headache?"

"Of course I have a headache. Someone slammed my head against a car." She tried to keep her words light, but her voice cracked on the last word.

Hayden swore softly before gathering her against his chest. He wrapped his huge arms around her and even though she knew it was a mistake, she slid her arms around him and laid the uninjured side of her head against his chest. That masculine, raw scent that drove her crazy twined around her, soothing her as much as his hold did. Right now she needed his strength and wasn't afraid to admit it.

"What do you know so far?" Hayden asked Jay.

"Someone wearing a black mask attacked her. She screamed, tried to run, and he caught up with her. Slammed her against that car," he said as he pointed to it. "It was just by chance I was down here too. I scared him off. I wanted to go after him but I couldn't leave her alone."

"I'm going to fucking kill him." There was such rage in Hayden's voice that Sierra stepped back. He was always in such tight control of his emotions, even when dealing with would-be thieves and criminals at the casino. Nothing ever ruffled him so to hear his voice practically shaking was a shock.

He wouldn't fully let her go though, sliding his hands lower and keeping them firmly on her hips. "Hayden, no, the police are on their way. They'll handle this. But I don't understand how anyone got in here. Unless..." Oh God, why hadn't she thought of that? It had to be an employee. "Someone from the casino did this?" An uncontrollable shudder snaked through her.

"Not necessarily," Iris said as she strode up. Sierra had seen her arrive with Hayden but the head of hotel security had been talking on her phone in hurried, but hushed tones. "I just got off the phone with one of the tech guys. Turns out there was a glitch in the system. Two of the doors down here were unlocked because of it and…the video feed was off too."

Sierra's blood chilled at the words. Next to her, Hayden stiffened, so she knew she wasn't crazy. The locks in the garage were electric so she could see a mistake happening if there was a computer error, but for the video feed to malfunction too… "The video just in this garage or everywhere?"

Iris cleared her throat. "Just this section of the garage."

Which meant this had been somewhat planned. Maybe she hadn't been the specific target, but the security at the Serafina was vigilant about having eyes everywhere, especially when it concerned the safety of their employees. It was one of the reasons Sierra loved working at the casino.

"I don't believe in coincidences," Hayden said.

Iris and Jay murmured an agreement as Sierra tried to wrap her mind around what had happened. It still seemed too surreal and she was just so damn grateful to be relatively unharmed. Things could have been a hell of a lot worse. Over the last month Sierra had fired multiple employees. Some for stealing, others for using drugs on the premises. It wasn't completely out of the realm of possibilities that someone had targeted her because of that. While she wanted to believe the best of people, she'd seen people do stupid stuff when they were desperate or felt wronged.

"I'm having a full systems check and analysis run on our security right now to figure out why we had a glitch with the locks. And you better believe I'll find out what happened to that feed. This kind of thing won't happen again," Iris said.

"I want all the names of the people Sierra fired since the opening of the Serafina. We'll focus on them first, and if we can't narrow it down we might expand our suspect pool." There was no denying the underlying rage in Hayden's voice. If anything, he seemed even angrier than a few moments before.

The sound of sirens getting near made Sierra wince, but she kept her focus on Hayden. "What about the police?"

"Tell them everything you know. They'll investigate but so will we. That fucker better hope the cops get to him first." He didn't look away from her as he spoke, a silent promise in his eyes that slightly terrified her.

Not because she was afraid of him. Sierra had always known Hayden was a badass. His military record was enough to prove that, but right now she felt like she was seeing him for the first time. Or at least the true warrior lurking beneath the surface. Before she could respond, Jay cut in.

"Shut it, Hayden. Don't let the cops hear you saying that shit," his brother muttered at the sound of screeching tires and slamming doors. Sierra looked toward the end of the row of nearest line of cars.

There were three marked and two unmarked police cars. A man she recognized as a detective from another problem they'd had at the casino strode toward them wearing a stony expression. Sierra wanted to bury her face against Hayden's chest and block everything out, but knew it was impossible. So she stepped back, ready to get the questioning and paperwork over with, but Hayden snagged an arm around her waist and pulled her close. His fingers dug into her hips, urging her to stay near.

Okay, then. She wasn't inclined to fight him, but she was surprised by his actions. Usually he was careful about not touching her too much. She sighed and sidled up next to him. The man was a complete rock, all hardness and muscles and raw strength. She could really feel it now too. Once all this insanity was ironed out she'd be going home alone so she wanted to take advantage of the support he was offering now.

"You finally going to make your move?" Jay asked quietly as he and Hayden stood near a concrete pillar out of the way of the police and the paramedics who were talking to Sierra.

Hayden crossed his arms over his chest, hating the helpless sensation he experienced as he watched Sierra shaking her head at something one of the paramedics said. Her arms were wrapped tightly around her middle and her shoulders were hunched, making her look even more fragile than normal. Her long midnight black hair was pulled up into a ponytail and after a long day of work she didn't have much makeup left. Even pale, tired and practically shaking, she was the sexiest woman he'd ever known. It wasn't just her looks—though there was no arguing she was beautiful, even if she didn't seem to realize it—she had the biggest heart of anyone he'd ever met.

When he'd started work at the Serafina, he'd had a chip on his shoulder the size of Texas. He'd been surly, not liking the direction his life had taken him. His brother Jay had left the Navy because a team of his men had died. Then Jay had gotten a job working directly for Wyatt Christiansen.

Hayden had left the Navy because he'd had to. And he'd been fucking pissed about it, even after he'd gotten such a prime position. He hadn't been grateful to find such a well-paying job close to his only family. No, he'd focused on the negative. Until he'd met Sierra. She'd told him to stop acting like a dick about something he'd said or done, and he hadn't been able to tell her to fuck off. He was a Southern boy through and through and never would have said that to a woman anyway, but Sierra had made him feel like shit. And he'd deserved it.

Everything had changed from that first meeting with her. It had been subtle at first, but now he was so damn grateful to be able to do another job he enjoyed. Working in the same vicinity of the woman he…damn, he couldn't even admit the words to himself. Rubbing the middle of this chest, Hayden realized Jay was staring at him.

"What?" he snapped.

"I asked you a question. You gonna make a move on her or what? There's a pool going on how long it's going to take you and if you wait another week, I'll win."

"Man, fuck you," he muttered, not missing the good-natured smile Jay gave him.

Hayden wasn't sure if his brother was joking about the pool or not, but there was one thing he knew for sure. He wasn't waiting any longer. After what had just happened to Sierra, he was letting her know how he felt.

"I'm not coming in tomorrow and neither is she. Probably not the day after either," Hayden said quietly, making sure no one overheard them. He knew it would take some convincing, but there was no way he was letting Sierra go home alone tonight. And forget about coming in to work tomorrow.

"You taking her back to your place?"

"Yeah...if she'll go."

"She will." There was a certainty in his brother's voice that Hayden didn't feel. "I know you want to be hands on with this, but Iris and the rest of the team have this covered. They'll find out what the hell is going on. In the meantime, Sierra doesn't need to be here. If this was a targeted attack on her..." Jay trailed off, not bothering to fill in what Hayden already knew.

Keeping her far away from the Serafina and under his roof was the smartest thing they could do for her.

When the detective and paramedics let Sierra go, he watched as she scanned the garage. She stopped when she saw him, relief lighting up her pale face. His body tensed with all her focus on him. "We'll leave her car here, but keep it under surveillance. I've got my phone. Call me for anything."

Jay grunted, likely because he or Iris had already planned to do just that. Hayden hurried toward Sierra, his shoes silent against the concrete. She still had her arms wrapped around her middle when she stopped in front of him.

"They're not making me go down to the station," she said, even though Hayden already knew they wouldn't. Normally it was protocol but Iris had called in a favor for Sierra. Something he greatly appreciated. "And I'm not going to the hospital. They can't do anything for me." The way she said it sounded as if she expected him to argue.

Hayden nodded because he understood. It was unlikely she had anything more than a mild concussion—and he didn't think she even had that. The bruising and swelling would heal on their own. "I don't blame you. Do you have everything you need to leave?"

Frowning, she nodded and patted her purse. "Uh, yeah."

"Good, you're coming home with me. We can stop by your place and grab a bag of clothes, but I'm not letting you out of my sight tonight. Your car will be safe here. Iris is going to keep it under surveillance."

Now Sierra's eyebrows rose. "Going home with you?"

"Yes."

She visibly swallowed, her expression confused. "Hayden, I appreciate the offer, but I'm fine going home by myself. I have a security system, so don't feel obligated or anything."

"Are you fucking kidding me?" He had to rein his temper in at her words. She'd just had a traumatic experience, but still. *Obligated?* He didn't think he'd done a good job of hiding his anger because she paled, making him feel like utter scum. Hayden scrubbed a hand over his face and took a deep breath. "Shit, Sierra, I'm sorry. I didn't mean to yell. I just...damn it, you were attacked. I need you safe."

To his surprise, she let out a low laugh.

"What?"

"I don't think I've ever seen you like this. Or heard you curse like, well, a sailor. Pun intended." The edginess that had been surrounding her seemed to fade a little. "So you're sure you don't feel obligated? Because I—"

He growled under his breath and palmed his keys. "Come on. We're leaving." Not caring what she thought, he took her hand in his. Those green eyes of hers widened, but she didn't struggle. Just linked fingers with him and silently let him lead her to the elevators. He was parked on another floor and couldn't get out of here soon enough. Part of him wanted to take over and lead the internal investigation, but being with Sierra right now was more important than anything.

It was beyond time he told her how he felt about her. If he lost her as a friend…no, he couldn't even go there. He wouldn't. He'd seen flashes of lust in her eyes before but the woman was so damn innocent. He was pretty sure she was a virgin even though she'd never come out and said it. He knew he wasn't remotely good enough for her, especially not if she was actually that innocent, but he wasn't waiting any longer. If she rejected him, he'd deal. If not…he was going to give her the most intense pleasure of her life. And make sure she enjoyed it so much she never wanted to walk away from him.

CHAPTER FOUR

Hayden tensed as he heard Sierra's light footsteps on the stairs. After stopping by her place and letting her grab enough clothes for a few days, they'd come back to his home. He lived in a two-story place next door to his brother in a quiet neighborhood on the outskirts of the city. He loved where he worked but he enjoyed being close to the desert at night. Everything out there was quiet, settled...the exact opposite of how he was feeling at the moment.

Sierra had wanted to take a shower so he'd decided to cook for her while she was upstairs. He'd had to grab chicken from his brother's house next door because he'd had nothing thawed out. He didn't remember making the simple rice and chicken mash up, though—because he'd been fantasizing about what she looked like in the shower. Naked, with hot water rushing over her delicious body. A body he'd fantasized about far too often. He imagined her nipples were—

"Hey, you cooked?"

He turned to find her stepping tentatively into his kitchen wearing green and blue striped pajama pants and a fitted green tank top. Unable to stop himself, his gaze zeroed in on her breasts. She definitely wasn't wearing a bra and he was at the end of his rope pretending he didn't feel anything for her. He simply couldn't do it anymore.

"Uh, Hayden?" Sierra's nervous voice drew his gaze up to meet hers.

She'd asked a question... "Yeah, I thought you'd be hungry." He turned back around and tried to will his body under control. Too bad it wasn't working. His cock was insistently pushing against the zipper of his pants, and he just prayed Sierra hadn't noticed.

"Thanks. Whatever it is smells amazing." She leaned against the counter next to him looking a lot better than a couple hours ago. Except that fucking bruise on her temple that made him want to hunt down her attacker and inflict serious damage. At least her ivory cheeks had color in them again and she didn't have that terrified look. She'd left her jet black hair down so that it fell in damp waves over her left shoulder, covering one breast. God, what he wouldn't give to taste her nipples. To suck on them until they were tight little buds, shiny from his kisses and—

Sierra laid a reassuring hand on his forearm and he realized he'd just been staring. "I'm okay. I hate that worried look on your face."

Hayden cleared his throat and turned off the stove, glad she'd mistaken his expression for worry. Ignoring her statement, he said, "I've got beer and water in the fridge—but you probably shouldn't have anything alcoholic tonight. It doesn't seem like you have a concussion but it would make me feel better. If I'd known you were coming I'd have picked something up. Luckily Jay had a few things at his place." His girlfriend Ellie's influence no doubt.

Sierra just smiled and pushed away from the counter. "I don't think I have a concussion either, but water is totally fine."

As Hayden pulled out plates he looked over his shoulder to find her bent over slightly as she peered into his refrigerator, that pert ass sticking up. The sight evoked way too many hot fantasies and he tore his gaze away with difficulty.

"Oh my god, pretty much *all* you have is beer and water. This is horrible, Hayden." Her sweet voice was chastising. "I would go crazy with a fridge like this. No wonder you're always eating at Cloud 9."

Grinning, he started to set the table. "They've got the best chef in town."

A beer and water bottle in her hands, she nudged the door shut with her hip. "Whatever. You can't live on just dinners of veal *forestiere* or roasted rack of lamb all the time."

"Yes I can. I already do."

She shook her head, but her lips curved up into a soft smile. "That's just sad. You need to take better care of yourself with meals like breakfast and lunch."

"How about I just take care of you tonight?" he murmured, watching her carefully.

Her cheeks flushed a delicious shade of pink as she sat at the table. "Thanks, I appreciate it."

He grunted, not wanting her appreciation.

"So have you heard anything from Jay or Iris? I know it hasn't been that long, but I thought they might have found something." She shivered lightly and Hayden resisted the urge to drag her into his arms and comfort her. He needed to show restraint when she was so vulnerable.

He shook his head as he set a plate of food in front of her. "Unfortunately, no. But give them time."

Compared to the masterpieces she created, chicken and rice was nothing, but it would fill her up and warm her body. So far she'd been handling everything well, but he was waiting for her adrenaline to crash. Before she fell asleep, he wanted her fed. So when she took a few bites but only pushed her food around with a fork, he frowned.

"Is it that bad or are you not hungry?" he asked before taking a sip of his beer.

"It's great, I'm just...I don't know what I am but I'm not really hungry. It's so sweet that you cooked for me.

I'm sorry I screwed up your plans tonight though." She said the last part in a rush and he didn't miss the flash of...hurt in her eyes before she masked it.

But that didn't make sense. "Plans?" He'd only had plans with her. Like every other Thursday for practically the past year.

"Your date." She set her fork down now, not even pretending to eat.

Hayden blinked at her. What was she talking about? "I didn't have a date—except with you. It's Thursday."

Now she looked confused. "Oh."

A few things suddenly clicked into place. "You thought I had a date tonight? Is that why you left the security floor upset earlier?" He'd planned to ask her about it, but then the shit had hit the fan and that had been the least of his concerns.

"I wasn't upset. I was mad you didn't just tell me. I wouldn't have wasted a trip up to the fiftieth floor if I'd known you had plans. But...you really didn't?" she asked, her voice shaking slightly.

The thought that he might have had a date upset her no matter what she said. He could see it written all over her pretty face. Putting his own fork down, he scooted his chair closer and turned her so that she was facing him directly. He was going to set the record straight. "I don't know who told you I had a date, but they were mistaken." Casino gossip was notoriously wrong so he wasn't surprised someone had come up with that bullshit. Practically everything got twisted out of proportion there. Hell, he'd heard that Sierra had hooked up with two of his security guys and he knew for a fact that wasn't true. "I haven't been on a date or fucked anyone since the week I met you."

Her eyes widened, probably because of his crude language, but he could tell the news pleased her. "Really?"

He nodded.

"Oh." She bit her bottom lip nervously.

"Aren't you going to ask me why?" He intentionally dropped his voice, willing her to take the verbal bait.

"Why?" It came out as a whisper.

He leaned closer, placing his hands on the arms of her chair, completely caging her in. That sweet jasmine and vanilla scent of hers wrapped around him. She licked her lips, probably out of nervousness, but it just turned him on even more. "Because I don't want anyone else but you. I'd rather use my own hand and imagine bending you over my desk while I masturbate than actually fuck anyone else."

Her mouth fell open a fraction at his admission so he took advantage. Going at her fast, he crushed his mouth over hers. There was no finesse in his kisses, just a primal need to possess her as his tongue danced with hers.

For a single moment Sierra tensed, but then she was on him. Taking him by surprise, she grabbed onto his shoulders and slid onto his lap, straddling him. As she moved over his erection, he groaned. She was compact with the right amount of curves and he loved the feel of her on top of him. Her breasts rubbed against his chest and even with the material between them, he could feel her nipples. Hating that clothes separated them from touching skin to skin, he cupped her backside and stood, bringing her with him.

She instantly wrapped her legs around him, but when he started walking out of the kitchen, she pulled back. He didn't pause as he made his way to the stairs.

"Where are we going?" Her voice shook a little, but not from fear. The hunger in her gaze set him on fire. The potency was nothing compared to the brief little flashes of need he'd seen from her before. Flashes he'd wondered if he'd imagined.

What he saw now matched his own desire. But he needed to be sure. "My bed because I need more room." So much more to do what he had planned. "We can take things as slow as you want when we get there," he said as they reached the top of the stairs. But he hoped not too slow. The need to taste all of her was consuming him.

Those expressive eyes widened but she nodded as she leaned into him. He took her mouth again, holding her body against his so fiercely he tried to order himself to loosen his grip. But he couldn't. Not yet. Holding her like this was too damn surreal. For a fucking year he'd made it a point not to touch her.

Because he'd known *this* would happen. One kiss from her and his control was completely shredded. Pushing open his bedroom door with his foot, he headed for the king sized bed he'd never brought another woman to. He hadn't lived here long before getting a job at the Serafina and after meeting Sierra, he'd known he couldn't be with anyone else.

Not when he wanted her so badly. The thought of touching another woman had just felt wrong. He attempted to be gentle as he laid Sierra on the bed, but it was hard when she kept her legs wrapped tightly around his waist and was grinding against him in the most sensuous manner. If their clothes were gone, they'd be fucking. Not sweet, gentle love making like she deserved. Fucking could come later, but he wanted their first time to be slow.

Somehow Hayden tore his head back from Sierra. Her eyes were heavy lidded and her mouth was swollen from their kissing. Her full lips parted as she watched him. "You want to stop?" She sounded nervous.

"Fuck. No." Yeah, real classy. He cringed at himself, but Sierra just let out a laugh, the sound reverberating through to him.

"Then what's wrong?" Her legs loosened around him as she spoke.

Panic set in that she'd changed her mind. "Nothing. I just want to slow down, which means you can't touch me." His words were ragged and uneven. If she was touching him, he'd fuck things up. Of that he had no doubt.

No, right now was all about her pleasure. Before she could ask him why, he reached up and took her hands from his shoulders. Gently, he guided her hands above her head. With a simple platform style bed set he didn't have a railing for her to hold on to or even tie her wrists to...but he would come back to that idea once she was more comfortable with him. Her fingers touched the smooth headboard as he held her wrists in place.

"Why can't I touch you?" she asked.

Opening himself up to anyone other than his brother was foreign, but he'd already opened up to her so much in the last year he decided to be honest. If she ripped his heart out later, he'd fucking deal with it. "Because you make me insane, Sierra. All you have to do is walk into a room and I get rock hard. I want to be free to touch and kiss every inch of you, but if you're touching me, I'm going to be inside you. Balls deep, fucking like I've wanted to do from the moment we met." He rolled his hips, pushing his cock against the juncture of her thighs with insistency. Man, he wished there wasn't any clothing between them.

She shuddered, her eyes growing even more heavy-lidded with lust. "From the moment…" She trailed off when he possessively cupped her breast. Even though she had a petite frame, her breasts were a little larger than a handful. He gently massaged it, lightly rubbing his thumb over her nipple.

"The *moment*. You're so damn sweet I knew I was no good for you." She started to protest but he placed a finger over her lips. "The only thing I want to hear out of your mouth is 'faster', 'slower' or 'fuck me harder, Hayden'." He'd never been a talker in the bedroom so he wasn't sure what had come over him. Okay, that wasn't true. The most primal part of him understood that Sierra would need this. At least at first. She needed reassuring words and he'd give them to her.

Then he would sink inside her and not stop until one of them passed out from pleasure. "Can you follow orders?"

"Maybe."

"That's not what I want to hear," he murmured.

"Too bad." Her lips quirked up as she slightly wiggled her hips against him and he realized she was teasing.

He pushed out a slow breath. Yeah, he definitely needed to relax. Right now he was wound too tight.

He didn't bother fighting his smile. "No touching," he growled softly before nipping her bottom lip and tugging it between his teeth.

In response, Sierra moaned and arched her back. She moved her hands but instead of trying to touch him, she laid them against the sheets and dug her fingernails into the bedding. She wanted to touch him so bad she ached for it, but damn his bossiness. She would follow his orders. This once.

Okay, the truth was, she'd probably follow any orders he gave her in the bedroom if it paid off enough. The ache between her legs bordered on painful. For reasons she didn't even want to think about, she was still a freaking virgin at twenty-two. That was all about to change tonight. And something told her that Hayden would make this a night to remember. She should probably tell Hayden she'd never done this before, but she didn't want him to stop.

She still couldn't believe how open and almost dirty he was being with her. Sierra loved this side of him. Even though he was one of her best friends, he'd always been respectful of the fact that she was a woman and watched his language. Now he wasn't holding *anything* back. And it was hot.

Hayden's big hands skimmed down to the hem of her tank-top. For a moment he teased the bottom of it before slowly pushing it up. She swallowed hard when reality set in that he'd be seeing her naked soon. Unlike her gorgeous sister and mother, she hadn't gotten any height or their amazing genes. And she definitely wasn't like the tall, lithe women she'd seen hanging onto Hayden at the casino.

"Hey, where'd you just go?" Hayden asked.

Blinking, Sierra realized Hayden was staring up at her. One of his hands was lightly gripping her hip and the other had pushed her top up, baring her belly. "Nowhere."

His eyes narrowed. "Don't lie. Not now."

Showing insecurity was so not sexy but he was right. Sierra didn't want to lie. "I'm just worried you won't like what you see." Even admitting it out loud made her feel stupid, but luckily he didn't.

Sitting up, Hayden wordlessly started unbuttoning his shirt. Sierra held her breath as he began baring so much skin to her. As he slid the shirt off, her gaze tracked over his chest, his rock hard eight-pack of muscles, down to the V... his fingers started working his belt, then the button of his slacks.

She tried to tear her gaze away to see his expression but she couldn't move. It was as if she was frozen, watching him slowly strip for her. Pushing off the end of the bed, he stood at the foot of it. His long, calloused fingers slowly pushed his pants down and she realized she was biting her lower lip in anticipation. He had on black boxer briefs but the visible bulge was huge. It made her suck in a breath. When he finally shoved the briefs down his legs, Sierra's inner walls clenched with unfulfilled need.

He wrapped a hand around his thick cock and stroked once. Her gaze shot to his. His blue eyes seemed almost brighter in the dim room as he watched her. She realized he was baring himself to her so she'd feel comfortable but she didn't want him stroking himself, she wanted to be the one touching him.

Sitting up, she pushed off the bed and came to stand in front of him. She shoved aside her insecurities and slowly lifted her top off. Bare to him from the waist up, she still couldn't shelve the nerves fluttering in her stomach. Until his hungry gaze landed on her breasts.

"Pale pink," he whispered. She didn't understand what he meant until his eyes met hers again. "I've been fantasizing about the color of your nipples for too damn long."

Before she could formulate a response—and she wasn't sure there was one—he dipped his head and sucked her nipple into his mouth. She slid her fingers through his dark brown hair, tightening her grip as he lightly used his teeth.

Too many sensations surged through her. Instinctively she arched into his mouth, wanting more. So much more.

She couldn't believe she was in Hayden's bedroom, doing things she'd fantasized about. And she knew they'd only gotten started.

Grabbing her hips, he moved them backward until she was flat on her back and he was stretched out over her. She didn't have much time to appreciate all that male strength before his head dipped again toward her breast. He let out a strangled groan as he swiped his tongue over one nipple, then moved to the other. Teasing her nipples with his tongue, he licked and laved the hardening buds with erotic little strokes that had her grinding against him.

She might not have much experience but she knew exactly what she wanted. Her panties were damp, her inner walls clenching with a need she knew Hayden would fix.

Groaning, she grabbed his shoulder with one hand and ran her fingers through his dark hair with the other. She didn't care what he said about no touching. That so wasn't happening unless he actually restrained her.

That thought was insanely hot. But only if it was Hayden tying her down. She grew even damper at the thought.

As he continued teasing her, he started blazing a path of hot kisses down her chest, then stomach until he reached the top of her pajama pants. Oh god, he wasn't going to…yeah, he was.

Hooking his fingers on her pants, he snagged her panties too as he tugged them down her legs and tossed them to the floor. Sierra felt a moment of insecurity at being completely naked in front of him, but it vanished when his big body shuddered.

Actually shuddered as he tracked her from her feet up to her face.

"You're beautiful," he murmured before pressing his hands on the inside of her knees, urging her to spread her thighs wider.

Part of her wanted to cover herself, but with Hayden kneeling in between her legs looking hungry for her, she savored being on display for him.

She knew what he was going to do, could see the determined look in his eyes, but nothing prepared her for when he buried his face between her thighs. Her hips vaulted off the bed as he sucked on her clit. The action was sharp and unexpected and sent a punch of pleasure to all her nerve endings. She'd touched herself before but nothing compared to having Hayden's mouth on her most intimate area.

Groaning against her, he pressed on her inner thigh when she tried to close her legs. As he gently teased and licked her clit, he drew one finger down the length of her wet slit. She was so wet she was a little embarrassed. But when he'd told her that he'd wanted her from the moment they'd met, it had turned her on like nothing else could.

When he pushed a finger inside her, her inner walls clenched convulsively around him.

"Fuck," he muttered against her.

She tightened around him, loving the feel of him inside her. Slowly, he pulled out, then pushed back in, over and over, the action rhythmic and wonderful. The way he played her body was perfect and a little maddening. She knew she was close to orgasm but she needed more stimulation. It wouldn't take much to push her over. Her body was primed with the need to come.

"Touch your breasts," Hayden ordered, barely stopping to talk between his strokes.

Cupping herself, she was nervous to touch herself in front of him, but she didn't even think to deny his demand. With her thumbs she began lightly rubbing her already aroused nipples. As he increased the pressure on her clit, her toes curled against the sheets.

"I'm going to come." She wasn't sure why she was announcing it. Lord, her entire body was going into sensory overload.

He made an incomprehensible growling sound that was almost triumphant. When he added another finger to her pussy, her hips bucked against his face as a sharp climax surged through her. Piercing all her nerve endings, the orgasm was way more intense than when she stroked herself.

Her stomach muscles tensed as she rode through wave after wave of pleasure. Grabbing the sheets beneath her, she moaned as he continued his delicious assault until finally it was too much.

She had to push his head away. The stimulation against her clit was becoming almost painful. She was worried he'd be offended, but he chuckled as he pulled back and sat up on his knees.

"That was amazing," she whispered, glad she could actually find her voice. She felt so relaxed she was surprised she'd managed that.

He crawled up her body and brushed a light, almost chaste kiss on her lips. "We're just getting started." That knowledge made her nipples tingle in anticipation. But to her surprise, he pulled back and slid off the bed. Before she could ask what he was doing, he gave her one of his half-smiles. "Just need to grab something from the bathroom."

Confusion settled in before she realized he meant condoms. Of course. Thankfully he was thinking straight because she had no intention of thinking for the rest of the night. All she wanted now was to feel and savor every single sensation of Hayden making her his.

CHAPTER FIVE

Hayden pulled out a box of condoms and breathed a sigh of relief when he realized they hadn't expired. His hand actually shook as he took one out. With the sweet taste of Sierra still on his lips, he was barely keeping himself under control.

But after feeling her tight pussy, he knew they needed to talk first. He'd guessed just from knowing her, but he was pretty sure she was still a virgin after feeling how tight she was. Holding onto the packet, he strode back into his bedroom to find Sierra sitting up with the sheet pulled up to her chest, covering her breasts. He didn't like that at all. But he did like the sight of her in the middle of his bed with rumpled hair and a clearly satisfied expression on her face.

Right where she belonged.

Her gaze tracked to his hard cock, then went to the condom in his hand. When she licked her lips in that adorably nervous way he was used to, he tossed the condom onto his nightstand and sat on the edge of the bed. It was a serious effort in control not to just jump her. He drew the sheet away from her because he wanted to see all of her. Even if the sight of her breasts was a huge distraction.

"I need to ask you something, honey," he said quietly.

"I think I know what and yes, I'm a freaking virgin." Sighing, she fell back against the pillow. Her breasts bounced softly with the movement, making his cock ache even more. Sierra covered her face with one arm and groaned. "Does that mean you want to back out of this?"

"Hell no." Never. He stretched out next to her and propped his head up on one hand while laying his other over her flat stomach.

She dropped her arm to look at him and he saw relief in her eyes.

"How is that possible?" he asked, still astounded. She was a decade younger than him, but twenty-two was still old enough to have had a few lovers. The thought of anyone else touching her made a raw possessiveness rear up inside him but he shoved it down. Now wasn't about that.

Shrugging, she placed her hand over his. He could see the pain in her eyes, but she held his gaze. "It wasn't one thing. During high school the few times I thought a guy was interested in me it turned out they wanted to date my sister."

Hayden's lips pulled into a thin line at the mention of her sister, Shae. He'd met her once and that was enough.

She was the polar opposite of sweet Sierra. "I bet she ate it up," he muttered.

Sierra blinked, but didn't respond. She just cleared her throat and averted her gaze for a moment. "I didn't really care that much about the opposite sex in high school anyway. I was so focused on graduating and getting into the Culinary Institute of America and boys weren't important. Then in culinary school I was on the fast track program. The little downtime I had, I wanted to spend with my friends. Living in New York was amazing and there was always so much to do. I guess I'm just not a one-night stand kind of girl. There was never an opportunity." When he frowned she rolled her eyes. "Okay, there were opportunities, I just never took them. I wanted my first time to mean something… Gah, you've totally changed your mind about tonight haven't you?" She started nibbling on her lower lip again.

Hayden's eyebrows rose. "*No.* Why would you ask that?"

She shrugged jerkily. "I don't know. Maybe because I have really limited experience and I know you have…a lot more."

He wouldn't deny that. When he'd been in the Teams getting laid had been easy when he'd been stateside. All he'd had to do was head down to a local bar filled with SEAL groupies and have his pick. Sex had always been about release though. A way to chase away the demons. Until he'd met Sierra. It was like he could divide his life into halves now. Before Sierra and after. "I don't care about that and neither should you. There's no one in my life except you. This thing between us—it's not casual for me." Those were words he'd never said to a woman. Never thought he'd want to say. Until Sierra.

She'd called him on his shit literally the first time they'd met. And the feisty woman had just looked so damn sweet when she'd done it, there'd been no way he could be rude to a woman like her. She was always going out of her way to be kind to people at work whether they deserved it or not. For some reason she liked to see the best in people. She'd definitely seen it in him.

She smiled softly. "Me neither." The exact words he wanted to hear. He pushed out a breath he hadn't realized he'd been holding.

There was such a raw vulnerability in her eyes that it was like a punch to his senses. Sierra was so funny, smart and incredibly talented that her being nervous now surprised him. But after meeting her sister a few months ago, maybe he should have realized. The woman was gorgeous to be sure, but nothing compared to Sierra.

Even though his cock was aching and he had the most beautiful woman naked and willing next to him, for some reason he wanted to talk. *Fucking talk.* He inwardly sighed. Sierra totally owned him even if she didn't realize it yet. Maybe he should shelve the conversation, but he wanted to know everything that made this woman tick. "When I met your sister a few months ago..." Before he'd even finished, she stiffened beneath his hand and went to pull the sheet back up. To cover herself.

Hayden grabbed it and shoved it off her. Now that she'd bared herself to him, there was no way he was losing sight of her sweet body. She made a protesting sound but he rolled over and covered her petite body with his. Her legs automatically wrapped around his hips, pulling him close. He settled against her, savoring the feel of her beneath him, all warm and soft. With his cock so damn close to her pussy it was hard to think straight but he needed to make one thing clear. "A few months ago when your sister blew into town, I saw a side of you that I never want to see again. You were a totally different person when she met up with us. You withdrew into yourself, as if you were afraid to outshine her."

Sierra had been stiff up until that moment, but she snorted. "Outshine?"

Hayden frowned. "Yeah. Anytime I mentioned one of your accomplishments or even talked about *you*, you shut me down. Your sister is pretty, so what? She's also an asshole. You're fucking beautiful inside and out and you're amazing. You're fucking *twenty-two* and head chef at Cloud 9."

Sierra's eyes widened. "I can't believe you just said that."

He rolled his hips, dragging his erection over her belly. He wanted to shift positions and move lower but once his cock touched her pussy, it would be over for him. "You are beautiful."

Now she rolled her eyes, frustration clear on her face. "Not that. I mean about my sister."

He shrugged. "I didn't like the way she treated you. She talked down to you and made you feel like shit. Siblings shouldn't do that. And you put up with it. I...It's why I left early that night. I couldn't stand seeing it and I knew I'd say something I'd regret if I stuck around. Fair warning; if that ever happens again, I won't sit back and watch."

She watched him carefully for a long moment, as if assessing him. It looked as if she might say something, but then she cupped his face with both hands and leaned up to kiss him. Relief slammed into him that she didn't care what he'd said about her sister. If Sierra wouldn't stand up for herself, he damn sure would.

Sierra didn't know when it had happened, but she'd completely fallen for this man. When he'd said this wasn't casual for him, she was relieved but she hoped that meant the same thing for him that it did for her.

But she wasn't going to worry about that. At least not at the moment. No, she was going to take exactly what she wanted. Hayden was right about her letting her family treat her wrong. Growing up with such a gorgeous sister and a mother who placed a priority on looks had taken a toll on her self-esteem. Moving away for school and developing her own circle of friends had made a huge difference in the way she looked at herself. Intellectually, she understood all that but when her sister had stopped in town for a few days, Sierra had felt like that chubby fifteen year old again. It hadn't helped that Shae had flirted mercilessly with Hayden.

He'd barely tolerated Shae. Something that hadn't gone unnoticed. She'd been secretly pleased, and had fallen for him a little more that night. Sierra just hadn't been sure why he'd acted the way he had.

Until now.

As she held his face in her palms, Hayden's hands started roaming her body in a way she'd only fantasized about. After the orgasm she'd just had, she wasn't sure if she could have another but she didn't even care.

She wanted to feel him inside her, to be completely possessed by this man. When one of his hands cupped her breast and began rubbing her already sensitized nipple, she arched her back, pushing into his grasp.

As his other hand cupped her mound and slid two fingers into her slick opening, she felt as if she could combust on the spot. Feeling that thickness inside her made her entire body tingle because she knew soon it wouldn't be just his fingers.

He pulled his mouth back from hers and she started to protest, but his lips trailed down her jaw to her neck and he lightly tugged her earlobe between his teeth all while continuing the soft thrusting of his fingers. When he added another, she instinctively arched her back again, enjoying the fullness of him stretching her body.

Reaching between them, she wrapped her hand around his cock, amazed by the thickness and heat. She wanted to touch all of him, to stroke him the way he was her. Even more, she wanted to pleasure him, to learn his body and what he liked.

He groaned against her ear, the sound almost guttural as his entire body shuddered under her hold. "No touching," he growled.

"I never agreed to that." She barely rasped the words out as she continued stroking him. Just the feel of him in her hand made her feel powerful and sexy.

The hand that had been cupping her breast suddenly moved and encircled her wrist. He sat back so he could look down at her, hunger on his face as he moved her hand away from his hard length.

"This might hurt the first time." He looked so stricken she couldn't fight a smile.

"I know." She didn't care because she knew it wouldn't last. So many times in school she'd worried that she was an idiot for waiting but now she was glad she had. No one could ever compare to Hayden. It just wasn't possible.

His expression softened before he leaned over and snagged the condom. After sheathing himself, he covered her mouth with his. As his tongue danced against hers, he settled between her thighs, his cock nudging her opening. She clutched onto his shoulders in an attempt to ground herself. He slowly pushed into her a fraction, then stopped, letting her body adjust to him.

With his size, she'd worried it would hurt but she was so slick, so turned on, her inner walls were tightening, just waiting to be filled by him.

Rolling her hips, she tried to force him to move deeper but he just laughed lightly against her mouth. His lips trailed lower once again, nipping and teasing until he found her aching breast.

Sierra slid her fingers into his dark hair, clasping his head as he flicked his tongue across her nipple. Almost simultaneously, he began rubbing her clit again in a slow motion designed to torture her, she was sure. His thumb and forefinger increased in pressure when his tongue did.

She shuddered and increased her grip on his head as more pleasure spiraled through her. Tightening her legs around him, she dug her heels into his ass. "I need more, Hayden."

The second she said his name, it was like something in him snapped free. She could still feel him keeping a tight rein on his control, but he finally pushed deeper, giving her what she needed.

Both his tongue and expert fingers kept up their teasing as he pressed into her, then pulled out. He pushed in deeper the next time. In and out, not deep enough to give her exactly what her body craved, but enough to push her right to the edge.

She hadn't thought it possible, but she was close to coming again. "I'm close," she whispered, unable to get out more than that.

Her inner walls clenched tighter and tighter, trying to draw him into her as he tweaked her clit. When he lightly pressed his teeth down on her hard nipple, the sensuous action set off her release.

As her climax slammed through her, Hayden thrust fully inside her. All the breath whooshed from her lungs as he buried himself deep. The pain was fleeting, mixed with the surging orgasm punching to all her nerve endings.

"Sierra," he groaned. Hayden buried his face against her neck, letting out a strangled moan as his thrusts grew harder and more unsteady.

Rubbing her breasts against his chest, she savored all the sensations overwhelming her as she tightened her grip on his head. She felt as if she was holding onto him for dear life as he continued pumping into her.

She felt his heat, his stomach muscles clenching and when he let out a strangled moan against her ear, a raw type of power filled her as he climaxed long and hard. Eventually his thrusting slowed, though his breathing was erratic as he pulled his head back to look down at her.

Staring into those blue eyes, she thought she could drown in them and not care. Before he could ask her if she was okay, she smiled, unable to stop herself. "That was amazing." He was still half hard inside her so she tightened around him, dragging a shudder from his big body.

"Yes it was," he murmured before kissing her lips. Even though the caress was light, it still felt as if he was claiming her in some way and she was more than happy to let him.

She just hoped that wasn't wishful thinking on her part because she had completely fallen for Hayden.

CHAPTER SIX

Hayden traced his finger down Sierra's bare stomach and grinned against the top of her head when she covered his hand with hers to stop him.

"That tickles," she murmured, still half asleep.

She was tucked up against him, her compact body snug and exactly where it should be. The feel of her ass right over his cock was driving him crazy, but it was worth it to have her in his arms. Now that he had her in his bed, he wasn't letting go.

In response he nipped her shoulder with his teeth then followed up with a swipe of his tongue.

"Oh my god, are you a morning person?" she groaned and wiggled against his erection. "Let me sleep, you maniac."

He chuckled, despite the ache between his legs. "It's almost noon."

She stiffened then turned in his arms. Her green eyes were bright with surprise. "Are you serious?"

"Yep." Hayden tightened his arm around her, pulling her close.

Her breasts rubbed against his chest as she wrapped her arms around him, making him shudder. He'd never get tired of the feel of her in his arms like this. It wouldn't take much to slide right into her, but he worried she'd be sore after last night. After their first time together he'd assumed she'd be too sore to do anything else but they'd made love again in the shower a few hours later. Thankfully he'd lasted a hell of a lot longer then. Getting inside her that first time had been electric. He'd felt like a fucking teenager barely able to control himself.

"I can't believe I slept so long," she murmured against his chest as she snuggled closer.

"A lot happened yesterday and we were up *very* late. You needed it." He slowly rubbed his hand up and down the length of her spine, enjoying the way she felt against him.

When he went to cup her ass, she laughed and pushed at his chest. "No. I need to brush my teeth and I'm starving." Almost on cue, her stomach rumbled, which made her cheeks flush that shade of pink that drove him crazy.

He could eat too, though he'd rather eat her. But after the day she'd had yesterday, he was taking care of her right now. The most primal part of him wouldn't allow any less. "Jay dropped off some groceries a few hours ago so come downstairs when you're ready." He threw off the covers and slid out of bed because good intentions or not, if he stayed there, he knew what would happen between them.

A soft smile played across her lips as her gaze tracked his movements. It roved over his entire body in a way that made his cock even harder. Something he hadn't thought possible.

"Keep looking at me like that and you're not leaving that bed."

Her eyes met his and he could tell she was contemplating just that. But...she needed sustenance. Groaning, he dragged on a pair of boxers and hurried from the room. The sight of her naked and willing in his bed was too much for his restraint.

Downstairs he started making turkey sandwiches. He was so thankful Jay had brought food over even if he was a little embarrassed by how bare his fridge had been. If he'd thought Sierra would be coming over he'd have made sure he was better prepared. At least his place was clean.

A few minutes later Sierra came downstairs looking refreshed and wearing one of his T-shirts. And nothing else. She was so petite it fell almost to her knees, covering more than some dresses he'd seen her wearing. Still, it would be so easy to push his shirt up and—

"No way." Sierra stepped into the room with a half-smile. Before he could ask what she meant she continued. "After last night I recognize that look very well and I'm hungry and...a little sore."

Guilt instantly flooded him but she crossed the short distance to where he stood at the counter. She went to wrap her arms around his middle and he tugged her close, embracing her tightly. "Sorry, I wasn't even thinking."

"I didn't even realize it until I got out of bed. I think I just need a few hours and I was thinking..."

"What?"

"I called my doctor and she can fit me in today. Since I have the next few days off I'd like to get a prescription for the Pill as soon as possible." She looked almost nervous as she said it. He couldn't understand why.

The thought of getting to be inside her with no condom made him shudder. "I'll take you."

"Really?" She seemed surprised.

"I'm not letting you out of my sight."

Worry slid into her eyes as she looked up at him and he knew she was thinking of the attack. "Have you heard anything from the casino?"

Hayden shook his head as he cupped her cheek and gently turned her face. Anger surged through him at the sight of her bruise. It was a little darker today, a faint purple staining her temple. "They're ripping apart the video feeds, trying to see if they can get another shot of the guy running away and Iris has brought in all new tech guys to comb over the system for glitches or signs of outside hacking."

"It seems like a lifetime ago," she murmured, laying her head against his chest.

"I hate that it happened to you." He slid his fingers through her hair, cupping the back of her head and holding her close.

"I do too, but I'm not sorry about what happened between us."

"Me neither." He hated that it had taken her being attacked to wake him up, but now that he had, he wasn't letting her go.

Sierra tossed a new toothbrush and tube of toothpaste into her hand-held basket. After going to her doctor, she'd dropped off her prescription for birth control at the pharmacist and had decided to wait the hour it would take for them to fill it instead of coming back. Hayden didn't want to wait, but he was just being difficult and it was silly to go all the way back to his house, then come back here. Yes, someone had attacked her at work, but unless he was keeping something from her, she doubted someone was stalking her and she refused to stop living her life.

It was a little odd to have Hayden with her though. She was so used to doing things on her own. "You don't have to hover," she murmured, unable to ignore his giant presence behind her as she tried to decide which shampoo she wanted.

She lightly nudged him with her elbow only to come in contact with pure muscle. He let out a pained sound. Immediately she turned and looked up to find him grinning at her.

Then his expression turned serious. "I just don't like having you out in public."

"It's not like there's an assassin hiding in the candy aisle." She nudged him again when his gaze immediately went in that direction.

He looked back and started to respond when his phone buzzed. "It's Iris," he murmured. "I need to take this."

As he slid his phone out, she mouthed the word 'restroom' and handed him her basket. He started to follow her, but she glared at him. She certainly did not need any help in there.

He held up a hand in a defensive gesture as he answered, but stayed put. Probably because he could see the entrance to the short hallway where the restrooms were.

Sierra hurried, not wanting to take the chance he might actually follow her in. The sexy man had been her shadow all day—which she appreciated. But there were some things she didn't need him for.

As she stepped inside the florally scented room with small square green tiles reminiscent of the seventies, she let out a sigh of relief. Being with Hayden all morning was wreaking havoc on her senses. The man was walking talking sex appeal and he was hers. At least for the moment. She was trying to wrap her head around her new relationship along with the craziness of yesterday. Before she'd taken another step, the closest bathroom door opened and her friend Marty stepped out. He worked in hotel security analyzing videos.

And he was pointing a gun right at her.

It was as if all the air in the small room was sucked out. For a moment all she could do was stare at the weapon and him. "Wh..." She cleared her throat, trying to find her voice. "What are you doing?"

His dark eyes narrowed, his face twisted into an expression of rage she'd never seen on anyone. "You're coming with me, slut."

That word was like a slap to her senses. "What?"

"You heard me," he growled, though he hadn't made a move closer yet. And his gun hand never wavered. Which told her he was pretty damn comfortable holding the thing.

Her insides quaked as she watched him, but she forced herself to remain outwardly calm. After working at one of the most stressful, busiest restaurants in the city, she was used to working under pressure. Of course her only pressure there was the fear of getting fired. Not losing her life. "Why are you pointing that at me? I thought we were friends. And how did you know I'd be here?" She remembered that he was the one who'd told her Hayden had a date.

He rolled his eyes and took a step closer. "I tracked you using your phone. Had to duck in here so your giant shadow wouldn't see me. Didn't know you'd come in here," he muttered. Before she could respond, he covered the few feet between them and grabbed her arm in a vise like grip as he shoved the gun into her side. She let out a tiny yelp of pain as his fingers dug into her skin.

An icy chill snaked through her veins, her entire body growing clammy. Even with the material of her summer dress as a barrier, the feel of the gun against her was surreal.

"You're coming with me." He pressed the gun deeper into her ribs, but she bit back a cry, not wanting him to accidentally shoot her. He pulled open the door and peered into the quiet hallway.

She couldn't see anything because of the angle he was holding her at, but the hall must have been clear because he let out a sigh of relief.

Sierra found her voice. "I'm not going anywhere with you." She was glad her voice didn't shake. She sounded a lot braver than she actually felt. Marty was clearly unstable, but if he'd been smart and determined enough to track her, he wasn't going to just shoot her in a public place. And there was no way in hell she was leaving this building with him.

He turned to look at her then, that look of rage so crystal clear it made her shiver. This was a man very capable of violence. It stunned her. How had she never noticed it before? "Unless you want me to fill you with bullets, you'll do exactly what I say."

CHAPTER SEVEN

Hayden stood at the end of the aisle of feminine products as he waited for Sierra, his phone against his ear. There was a security mirror angled on the far wall so he had a perfect view of the hallway without letting her or anyone else see him. He didn't want her to feel smothered by his presence but he still wasn't letting her out of his sight.

He understood that she wanted to get back to normal and that was why he'd been okay with bringing her to the doctor and now to the pharmacy. Maybe 'okay' was a bit of a stretch, but she couldn't stop living because of one lone maniac.

Or at least that's what he'd thought until what Iris had just said to him over the phone. "Both you and the police are sure Marty is behind this?" he asked. The thought of someone Hayden had actually worked with being involved made him see red.

"Unfortunately yes. He didn't come into work this morning and the outside team I've got combing through his online tracks all point in his direction. Thanks to a weakness in the system he was behind the glitches in the security. Luckily we've been able to create a new patch to prevent this issue from happening again."

That was good, but Hayden was more concerned about what was being done to find this maniac. Slamming Sierra's head into a car could have caused serious damage, potentially even killed her. "What about Vegas PD?"

There was a short silence then Iris cleared her throat. "They've searched his place and...you're not gonna like it, but they found a creepy shrine to Sierra. He's clearly obsessed with her."

Hayden scrubbed a hand over his face. A stalker type. Fucking great. "He wasn't working alone." Marty had been in the security room when the attack had gone down and he'd been the one to cause the glitch. He'd probably expected to be able to cover his tracks immediately. Maybe he and whoever he'd been working with had wanted to abduct Sierra and no one would have been the wiser if not for Jay being there to stop the attack. That seemed more likely if the guy was obsessed.

"Yeah, too bad there's no trace of a partner at his home. The cops are tearing his place apart as we speak, trying to find—"

"Shit," Hayden muttered. All the air rushed from his lungs as he watched Marty step out of the bathroom holding Sierra close. Hayden instinctively stepped back and crouched behind the nearest aisle. He felt as if he'd just been punched in the stomach, but managed to keep his initial spike of fear in check.

"What?" she demanded, her tone sharp.

"Marty just walked out of the bathroom with Sierra. I can't see a weapon but he's got to have one." How the hell had he tracked her without Hayden noticing? Sierra was stiff, her back ramrod straight as Marty dragged her down the hall to where Hayden knew was an exit.

Hayden couldn't see her expression because of the way she was being propelled along, clearly against her will. The man was about five feet ten. With Sierra's petite frame, he towered over her and would easily be able to manhandle her. The guy had to have a weapon. No way would Sierra be walking out with him otherwise.

Hayden was armed and ready. He rarely left home without a gun on his person, but with what had happened with Sierra, he'd made sure he was prepared for anything. "Call the cops. Give them my location." He rattled off the name of the store and major cross-streets before he ended the call and slipped it into his pocket. There wasn't much time to formulate a plan. He had to act now or risk losing the woman he loved.

Marty hurriedly looked over his shoulder, but didn't even glance upward in the direction of the mirror as he headed for the back door. Since he couldn't see anyone he assumed he was safe.

That bastard was about to find out the hard way he was far from it. And if he hurt Sierra, he would pay.

Even though everything inside Hayden was urging him to race after them, he knew he had to play it smart and head out the front, then circle back. If Marty had a partner it was possible the guy was waiting outside and armed as well. Hell, probably.

Hayden rushed out of the front door, quickly scanned the parking lot for another threat then immediately headed west to the quietest side of the building. They'd be in the back by now and he had only seconds to get to her. On the east side there was a pet store. Peering around the corner of the building, he could see the back half of a black SUV peeking out. Behind him there were the normal sounds of the street; cars, people walking their dogs and talking on their phones but all of that faded into the background as he zeroed in on his target.

Calling on all his strength, he sprinted down the side of the building, his legs quickly eating up the distance. Weapon drawn from his ankle holster, he paused at the very end of the building.

"You can shoot me because I'm not getting in there!" Sierra's terrified voice rolled over him.

Peering around the corner, he saw Marty trying to drag Sierra to the back passenger door of the idling SUV. The windows were tinted too dark—illegally so—

to see if anyone was inside but Hayden didn't doubt he had someone else behind the wheel.

Only ten feet away and hidden, it was still too far for comfort. Hayden's blood rushed in his ears as he mentally prepared himself for what he had to do. The moment Marty took his gun off Sierra, Hayden was making his move.

He'd killed in the line of duty before and right now, he knew nothing was more important than protecting this woman. His woman.

Marty held a gun pressed to Sierra's ribs but she was still struggling. She dug her feet in, trying to pull away from him. When the back door opened, without loosening his grip Marty moved his gun hand to grab for the handle.

Stepping out from around the corner, he raised his SIG. "Drop your weapon!" Hayden shouted.

Marty's gaze snapped to his, the intent clear in his eyes as he started to raise his weapon.

Hayden took the only opening he might have. No way was he letting anyone take Sierra or use her as a hostage. He fired at Marty. His training kicked in as he aimed and shot right at the man's chest. Three shots right in the center.

He was aware of Sierra throwing herself to the ground as Marty dropped like a stone. Unlike bullshit Hollywood movies, he didn't fly back through the air, just died where he stood. Immediately Hayden turned his weapon in the direction of the vehicle.

A man wearing a black T-shirt and black cargo pants had his hands raised in the air as he fell out of the side door he'd been attempting to open from the inside. He stumbled and landed on his knees. "Don't shoot! I'm unarmed! I'm unarmed!"

He would believe that after he'd checked the guy himself. "Sierra, kick Marty's weapon away." Hayden was almost positive the man was down, but he wouldn't take any chances.

He couldn't see her expression because his attention was on the second man, but Hayden watched out of the corner of his eye as she picked up the gun.

The back of the building was clear except for a large green Dumpster. "Keep your hands on your head," he ordered the man as he approached, weapon still trained on him. With Sierra safe and unharmed, all his focus was on this remaining threat. The guy was on his knees and trembling as if he might piss himself. In the distance, Hayden heard sirens as he patted down the unknown man.

When he was sure the man had no weapons, Hayden ordered him to lay face down on the concrete and keep his hands stretched out so they were visible. Keeping an eye on the guy, his weapon still trained on him, he stepped sideways in Sierra's direction. He risked a quick glance at Marty's prone body. Chest wasn't moving and blood was pooling all around him.

Out of the corner of his eye Hayden could see Sierra trembling as she stood there, tightly gripping the fallen gun in her hand. Reaching out with his left hand, he took it from her and tucked it in his waistband at his back as he closed the few feet between them. "Sweetheart, how are you? Did he hurt you?" He didn't want to take his eyes off the downed man for a second, not even to fully give her a visual scan.

"He didn't hurt me but he was going to." She wrapped her arms around herself so he threw an arm around her shoulders and dragged her close, still keeping his gaze on the other man. Marty was definitely dead. The cops would verify it when they got there.

"You're safe now," he murmured, wishing there was more he could do other than stand around and wait.

The sirens grew louder and when he was fairly certain they'd pulled into the parking lot, Hayden tucked his gun away. The man on the ground was still shaking in fear, his face turned away from them so he couldn't see what Hayden was doing.

When the cops arrived on the scene, he didn't want to be holding a gun. Even if he'd done nothing wrong, he knew what would happen if his weapon was displayed.

"We're all going to have to go down to the station and you're going to have to answer a lot of questions. Me too. They'll likely separate us to make sure our stories match but video cameras inside back us up and Marty is already a wanted man." They'd done nothing wrong but it wouldn't hurt to have video evidence on their side.

She started to ask something but he just shook his head when two uniformed police officers rounded the building with weapons at the ready.

Now wasn't the time to tell her about Marty's obsession with her. She'd get her answers soon enough. And he wanted to get her away from the dead body and into the safety of a police station as soon as possible. He wanted answers about who this accomplice was and what their plans for Sierra had been.

A raw type of rage was pumping through him that he'd never experienced before. Holding her close helped soothe it, but he couldn't get the image of her being held at gunpoint out of his head. Didn't know if he'd ever be able to erase that nightmare.

Sierra jumped at the sound of Hayden's doorbell ringing and almost spilled her wine. It was nearing midnight and she was emotionally exhausted. After spending most of the day at the police station answering questions and filling out reports, she and Hayden had finally been let go. She knew she should go to bed, but she'd been enjoying just curling up in his arms and relaxing. After what he'd done for her, she was worried about him too. He seemed totally fine with killing someone to protect her and she wasn't sure how to bring up her concern for him.

She set her glass on his side table and Hayden slid her off his lap onto the couch. "Who is it?" she whispered even though there was no possible way anyone else could have heard her. He'd received a couple texts over the past hour so she was guessing his brother.

"Either Jay or Iris. Stay here," he said in that familiar commanding voice before leaving the room.

Under normal circumstances she might have argued at his bossy tone but after the day she'd had, she didn't care. And she knew he was just looking out for her.

Sierra heard the murmur of multiple voices then a few moments later Iris and…holy crap, Wyatt Christiansen walked into Hayden's living room holding Iris's hand. Sierra was wearing yoga pants and one of Hayden's T-shirts that was a couple sizes too big. He'd insisted she put it on because he liked her in it, but staring at the mega billionaire she felt self-conscious. He was technically her boss, but it wasn't like she ever saw him.

Why was he here? Sierra stood and looked from Hayden to Iris with curiosity.

Hayden immediately crossed back to her and wrapped an arm around her shoulders. His presence was more than comforting. She felt like she could take on anything with him by her side. "Is everything okay?" she asked, looking at Iris. Sierra briefly wondered if she was going to get fired or something. She couldn't imagine why but why the heck was Wyatt Christiansen here?

As if he read her mind, the tall man with midnight black hair and piercing blue eyes gave her a half-smile. "I was out of town on a trip when you were attacked. Iris has filled me in on the details and I wanted to assure you that this kind of thing won't be tolerated in any of my casinos. We run extensive security checks, but Marty had never been convicted of anything and there were no red flags. Still, I'm sorry about what happened to you and wanted to let you know that you can take off as much time as you need to adjust to everything and we'll be paying for counseling if you decide you'd like it."

Wow. Sierra hadn't thought that far ahead and she doubted she would need any counseling. She was almost embarrassed to admit that she wasn't sorry Marty was dead. He'd been a monster. But the offer was generous.

Before she could respond, Christiansen continued. "There's no time limit on that offer. If you decide a year from now you want counseling, set it up and we'll take care of it."

"Thank you. That's very kind." Sierra tightened her grip around Hayden, feeling near her breaking point. She just wanted to be alone with him and decompress.

Iris motioned to the loveseat. "Mind if we sit?"

Hayden murmured an agreeable sound then they all sat, facing across from each other. There was obviously more to this visit.

Iris leaned slightly forward, sitting on the edge of the seat. Wyatt leaned back against the loveseat, and Sierra imagined the man would be comfortable anywhere. His hand rested casually at the small of Iris's back in a possessive gesture. "I could have called," Iris said. "But I wanted to let you know all this in person. Hayden has been cleared of the shooting, not that there was ever a fear he wouldn't be. Marty's partner got a lawyer and tried to cut a deal but with Marty dead and since Nevada is a three-strike state—Terry Hess will be going to jail for a long time. He confessed to being hired by Marty to attack you at the Serafina, then to helping him attempt to kidnap you today. About a month ago it seems Marty overheard a friend at Cloud 9 joking with you about…"

Iris cleared her throat, clearly uncomfortable, "…you being a virgin. I guess he became obsessed with you and well, wanted you. He paid Terry a lot of money to help him kidnap you. We'll never know what sent him over the edge but I'm guessing your relationship with Hayden played a factor." She pushed out a long sigh. "Personally, I don't give a shit what that lunatic's reasoning was. I'm just glad he's dead."

Sierra wasn't surprised by the other woman's bluntness. But she wished she could feel more relief. She felt some, for Hayden's sake. She was so thankful he was cleared of the shooting. "Will I have to testify?" She'd do it, but the thought of seeing that man again, especially knowing he was the one who attacked her in the parking garage was intimidating.

Iris shook her head. "No, he admitted to most of his crimes in exchange for waiving a jury trial. It shaved a few years off his sentence, but not many. I don't think he wanted to risk going away for longer than twenty-five years."

Now real relief surged through Sierra. That was a long time. "Thanks for letting us know in person."

Iris nodded and stood, her husband following suit. "Take the next week off. I've already got you covered at the restaurant." Sierra started to protest but Iris shook her head. "I'm not asking. You too, Hayden. I don't want to see either of your faces at the casino unless you're there to enjoy yourself."

To Sierra's surprise, Hayden quickly agreed and tightened his grip around her shoulders. After they said their goodbyes and walked the couple out, Sierra once again found herself in Hayden's lap on the couch.

He nuzzled her neck, lightly kissing that sensitive spot behind her ear. "Even though I want to take you right here, I think it's time for bed. You need rest."

She lightly pushed his shoulder, making him look at her. "You need it just as much as me. But first...are you okay with what happened?"

His eyebrows pulled together in confusion. "I hate what happened to you."

"No, I mean, killing Marty." It felt weird to even say the words.

His expression immediately cleared, but he paused and she could see that he was choosing his words carefully. "I'm not sorry he's dead and I won't suffer from any guilt over killing him if that's what you're worried about. I did what I had to in order to protect you and I'd do it again."

She was tempted to ask him if he was sure, but she could see the truth in his eyes. They'd talked about his Navy career many times and though he'd never been able to tell her much about his missions, she realized now that he'd killed in the past. She'd figured he had, but now she knew without a doubt. Considering how much he'd given for his country, she was more than okay with that. Seeing death up close and personal had jarred her and it wasn't something she ever wanted to experience again, but she didn't want to talk about that right now. If he could deal with it, she could too. "Okay."

He continued looking at her, an intense expression on his handsome face. "I love you," he blurted.

She blinked.

Before she could even think of a proper response, he continued. "I know it's the wrong time and probably too soon for you, but it's true. I've felt this way for a long fucking time. Since about two months after we met."

Sierra blinked again. "Why didn't you say anything then?" The words came out louder than she'd intended, but Lord, she'd been harboring a crush on this man since the moment she'd met him. And she felt the same way too. Especially now.

"I...didn't think I was good enough for you. I knew you were pretty innocent and I was still trying to transition to civilian life. You remember what I was like," he muttered.

She laughed lightly. "Yeah, you were kind of a bear to be around."

"And you were the only one to call me on it. At first I was just insanely attracted to you. You wouldn't believe the fantasies I had about fucking you at Cloud 9 after hours."

Sierra's face heated at his words because she'd had more than a fantasy or two about him too. Probably not as dirty as his though. "I love you too, Hayden. I—"

Whatever she'd been about to say was lost as he crushed his mouth over hers. As his tongue danced with hers, she wrapped her arms around his neck. Thoughts of sleep and the insanity of the past couple days faded to nothing when she was with him. After everything that had happened, she was right where she wanted to be. Safe and in Hayden's arms.

CHAPTER EIGHT

One week later

At the sound of Hayden's front door opening, Sierra slid the covered pan into the pre-heated oven and pressed start on the timer. She'd done all the prep work early so this would be ready to go as soon as he returned. It would give them an hour and a half until dinner was ready. There was plenty she wanted to do in that timeframe.

She was a gourmet chef, but for the last week he'd pretty much refused to let her do *anything*. Well, unless it involved her being naked, and cooking without clothes wasn't something she was brave enough to try yet. The traditional style beef pot roast was incredibly simple but she'd spiced it up just a little. He ate at Cloud 9 all the time so she had no doubt he'd like the meal.

But she hoped he liked her surprise even more.

"Sierra?" Hayden called out in that voice that made her toes curl.

"In the kitchen." She kept her back to the entryway, but looked over her shoulder, wanting to see his expression. Wearing just heels and a dainty little apron—which she'd changed into after prepping the meal—she'd wanted to do something fun for him tonight. It was a small apron, the square front cut barely covering her nipples and it was all lace and ruffles. Totally impractical for actual use, but she hoped Hayden found it sexy.

He'd had to stop by work to go over his schedule and to head up a meeting regarding next week's security plans. It was standard for him, but for the last week they'd been so wrapped up in each other he had a lot of catching up to do. And that was because of her. Not that she felt guilty or anything, but still...

Hayden stepped into the doorway, his tie loosened and his button down shirt undone at the top. With a bouquet of flowers in his hand, he started to smile then froze, his arm falling limply to his side as he took in her outfit. The apron tied in a neat bow at the middle of her back but he could see pretty much all of her backside.

"Holy shit," he growled.

She loved that she got that reaction out of him. Turning to face him, she didn't bother fighting a smile as his gaze skated over her from head to toe. The way the black and white ruffled apron fell, it just barely covered her breasts. Walking toward him, she'd only taken two steps when he covered the distance between them in long, determined strides.

He dropped the flowers on the table before grabbing her hips and hoisting her up. Familiar with what he wanted, she wrapped her legs around his waist, plastering herself to him as he claimed her mouth in a hungry kiss that had her arching into his rock hard chest.

Surprising her, he pulled back after a few intense moments. Dazed, she blinked. "Why are you stopping?" She'd been thinking about this from the moment he'd left.

"I swore I wouldn't jump you the second I got home." His voice was raspy and oh so sexy.

Sierra laughed lightly. "Why not?"

"I feel like all I've done is keep you naked the last week."

"And that's a bad thing?" Starting to feel self-conscious, she loosened her legs but he reached back and gripped her calves to hold her in place.

"No, I just wanted tonight to be special and…move in with me. Please," he added.

Her eyes widened but her grin grew. "Okay."

Now it was his turn to blink. "Okay?"

"You want me to argue?" It would have happened eventually and his place was huge and…she loved him.

"No, but I had a whole list of reasons prepared why you should."

She let out a bark of laughter. "Always ready for everything," she murmured.

Hayden instinctively tightened his grip on her smooth legs, then slid his hands back around until he cupped her ass.

When he'd seen her standing at the stove practically naked and her ass framed by the opening at the back of the apron, that familiar wave of possessiveness and love had welled up in him. He felt it every time he saw her.

It was jarring, foreign and...perfect. She'd filled a hole inside him he hadn't even realized existed. Making the transition to civilian life had been the hardest thing he'd ever done. Somehow she'd made it easier, just by being herself. He couldn't imagine his life without her. Didn't want to.

Now that he'd finally surrendered to his feelings for her and they'd crossed over from friends to lovers he knew there was no going back for him. The fact that she'd agreed to move in so quickly soothed the most primal part of him. Because he wanted a hell of a lot more from her than that.

He wanted forever. It was too soon to ask the big question just yet, but by Christmas of this year, he was going to make sure a diamond ring was on her left hand ring finger. He wanted the whole world to know she belonged with him.

Too soon, he reminded himself as he skimmed his hands over her bare ass. He shuddered at just the feel of her smooth skin and lightly squeezed her. When he did, she moaned into his mouth. The woman was so reactive and he couldn't get enough of her. He pulled back, and she opened her eyes.

"Bend over the island," he barely managed to rasp out.

Her green eyes lit up with desire at his words. She let her legs drop and though he missed the feel of her wrapped tightly around him, he was dying to take her from behind. For the past week he'd tried to be as careful and gentle with her as he could. But her bruising had almost completely faded and he was hiding behind that excuse anyway. She wasn't some breakable, fragile thing.

Sierra was one of the emotionally strongest women he knew. Yeah, she had insecurities like everyone else on the fucking planet, but she kept it together like no civilian he'd ever met. After the shooting he'd expected...something different from her. But she'd been so composed about the whole thing and that by itself, was hot.

"You're trying to kill me," he managed to rasp out as she bent over the marble island and pushed her ass toward him, grinning cheekily over her shoulder at him.

"You love it," she murmured.

He did. The sexy getup she wore stunned him. He'd never expected to come home and find her wearing nothing but an apron and fuck-me heels. It only reaffirmed what he knew about this woman. She was going to keep him on his toes. Keeping his gaze on her, he slowly undressed. First with his shirt and tie, then his shoes and pants. He'd gone commando because he'd known he'd be coming home to her. Her eyes tracked his movements and each article of clothing he lost, the heavier that gaze grew.

"I'll try and be gentle," he said as he gripped one of her hips and slipped a hand between her legs from behind. He dragged a finger down her slit and found her slick with need.

"I don't want that." Turning away, she let her head fall forward, her inky dark hair falling down her back in seductive waves.

"What do you want?" he asked quietly, smoothing his hand down the length of her spine. With her bent forward in such a submissive pose, his cock throbbed almost painfully. He pressed a finger into her, closing his eyes when she tightened around him.

She didn't respond, just pushed back, trying to get him to move. He slipped another finger inside her tight sheath, loving how she molded around him.

Sometimes he liked to tease her; other times he enjoyed getting her off quickly. Tonight he had a feeling it would be the latter. While he wanted to drag out the foreplay, he needed inside her like he needed his next breath.

"Need in you." He couldn't even formulate a complete sentence.

Sierra didn't seem to notice, just rocked against his fingers, her breathing growing erratic the faster he moved. He couldn't believe how primed she was, as if she'd been thinking about this all day. Maybe she had. God knows he had. He'd hated going into work, even for a few hours.

Without warning, he withdrew his fingers.

She let out a yelp of frustration, her fingers clawing at the marble top. "Don't tease." Instead of sounding demanding as he guessed she intended, her words were breathy and needy.

Feeling almost frantic, he retrieved a condom from his discarded pants and quickly sheathed himself. Until her birth control kicked in, he'd be using these but he couldn't wait to feel her pussy tightening around his naked cock. The thought of being inside her without any barriers was almost enough to push him over the edge, so he reined himself back in.

Until he guided his hard length to her wet opening. Feeling her wetness on the head of his cock was too much.

He pushed forward in one hard thrust. She was so wet, but let out a gasp as he buried himself in her tight body. Though he wanted to move, he was so damn primed right now. He wanted to make her come, wanted to feel her climaxing around him.

Staying buried inside her, he slowly pulled the bow from her apron free. He'd noticed that she was sometimes self-conscious about her body, so the fact that she'd been waiting for him, practically naked under the bright lights of the kitchen, told him how much she trusted him. That she was okay being vulnerable in front of him.

Thank God because he would give anything to make her happy. As the apron strings slid away, he reached up and lifted the part that secured around her neck over her head, letting it fall to the ground.

Sierra, bent over and waiting for him to fuck her. Wearing just sexy heels.

He didn't think there had ever been anything sexier. Yeah, his brain was going to short circuit any second now.

Sliding his hands up her hips and over her ribs, he only stopped when he was cupping her breasts. She was practically trembling, her body shaking with a need he understood all too well. Just lightly enough to tease her, he flicked his thumbs over her nipples.

"Faster, harder," she demanded on a breathless moan.

He wasn't sure if she meant his fingers or his cock and he couldn't make his throat work enough to ask. Strumming one of her nipples with more pressure, he let his other hand slide lower as he started thrusting inside her.

His movements grew harder with each drive into her tight body. Her inner walls clenched around him, growing tighter and tighter the harder he slammed into her. She was so close. He could feel it.

So was he, but he was desperate to make her come first. Tweaking her clit between his thumb and forefinger, he increased the stimulation on her sensitive bundle of nerves with just the right amount of pressure to push her over the edge.

"Hayden." The way she said his name was almost like a prayer as her the orgasm surged through her. Her body shook and trembled and she cried out even more loudly as she came.

He wasn't far behind her, his own climax hitting him like lightning, the pleasure pumping to all his nerve endings until finally he was just blindly thrusting his hips against her. Forcing himself to stop, he gently held her hips as he pulled out.

She made a soft protesting sound but barely moved a fraction while he disposed of the condom. When he was done, he turned her around to face him, pleased by the sated expression on her face. "I love you," she whispered, wrapping her arms around his neck and pressing her soft breasts against his chest.

"I love you, too." He'd never get tired of saying it, either. Holding her and being held by her was the best feeling in the world, and he was never letting her go.

CHAPTER ONE

Ellie shifted from foot to foot on the cold stoop, waiting for Sierra to answer the door. It was too cold to walk in slippers, even just to go next door. Vegas weather liked to keep her on her toes like that. October was a transitional month from pool to sweater weather, but there was nothing transitional about the chill snaking through her right now. It had to be in the forties or fifties.

As Sierra opened the door, Ellie rushed inside, keeping her arms wrapped around herself. She'd walked over from next door where she lived with Jay and hadn't realized how chilly it was outside.

"Jeez, what the hell are you wearing?" Sierra asked, taking in Ellie's thin sleep T-shirt, shorts and pink slippers.

"I didn't know it was cold outside. Jay is a freaking furnace and I grabbed this off the floor. I thought I'd sneak over before he woke up so I could snag a couple eggs. Please tell me you have some." Ellie was pretty certain she did. Sierra was only twenty-two, but she was head chef at Cloud 9, which was part of the Serafina, the casino owned by billionaire Wyatt Christiansen who they all worked for. Ellie was Wyatt's personal assistant and oversaw a lot of his businesses. She spent a lot of time working from her office at the casino since it was so new.

Sierra snorted as if the question was ridiculous. "Come on." She motioned toward the kitchen. "Hayden's a furnace too. Must run in the family." Sierra was living with Jay's brother—they'd just moved in together. "What are you making?"

"Just an omelet with a side of bacon. I wanted to cook a quick breakfast for Jay since I know he's got meetings all day." Jay was basically Wyatt's right hand man and head of his personal security. Wyatt wanted him interviewing possible new security guys for his own team and for a couple of his other establishments. She understood why too. As a former SEAL Jay was good at seeing through bullshit and assessing things you just couldn't get from a resume. He would be able to gauge whether these interviewees would be a good personality fit. All the experience in the world wouldn't matter if someone was a grade A asshole.

"So fancy," Sierra murmured, unhidden laughter in her voice as she opened the fridge.

"Ha, ha. Whatever Miss Fancy Pants, I don't want to hear it. The man is lucky he's getting any breakfast at all." It was no secret she didn't cook well. But Ellie *knew* she couldn't screw up eggs and bacon.

Sierra snickered as she handed her the half empty egg carton. "I don't know if lucky is the term he'd use."

Ellie's eyes widened at the unexpected joke from Sierra. "If I hadn't started a tiny fire the last time I used the kitchen, I might be insulted."

Sierra stifled another laugh. "Do you want a sweater?"

"Nah, I'm just running back over there. Thanks again." Once outside she hurried to the house she now shared with Jay. Unlike Sierra, who had moved in with Hayden after a couple weeks, it had taken Ellie months to officially move in with Jay. During the months he'd been recovering from an explosion meant to kill their boss she'd practically lived here, but once he was on his feet and back at work, she'd kept her own place for almost half a year.

It wasn't that she didn't love him, because she did. More than anything. But moving in with someone was a big deal. She and Jay already saw each other all the time because of their jobs and she'd been worried about losing her limited amount of personal space. Plus, she'd kept waiting for the other shoe to drop. She'd been convinced that what she had with Jay was too good to be true. That it was all going to end if she got too happy with him. Because that's how life worked in her experience.

And the intuitive man had known, had called her out on it once and told her to accept that he loved her and wasn't going anywhere. She knew that in her heart, but it was so damn hard getting her head to line up with that knowledge. At least he hadn't pushed her. Ellie knew Jay wanted more from her—as in, 'til death do us part—but he was never pushy about anything. For that, she was grateful. It just solidified how right he was for her. Hell, how right they were together. They definitely balanced each other out. Lord knew he balanced out her neurotic tendencies.

Once inside their two-story home, she shut and locked the door behind her. Out of habit, she put the alarm back on stay mode. That was the one thing she and Jay were both vigilant about. Of course he had his own version of security with his trusty SIG and his SEAL training. The man definitely knew how to take care of himself. And her—in more ways than one.

Her chill started to fade as she made her way to the kitchen. The second she stepped inside she found Jay leaning against the countertop, steaming coffee mug in hand, and the cold disappeared altogether. At six foot, five inches, with a skull trim haircut, and sleeves of tattoos covering his arms, he made her mouth water. Especially since he was only wearing boxers.

He started to give her one of those wicked smiles that melted her insides but it quickly turned into a frown as he raked a concerned gaze over her. "Were you next door? It's freezing outside."

"How was I supposed to know that? It's not even cold in here." Which was weird. She hadn't felt the cold because Jay was so warm at night.

"I turned the heater on around midnight when you shivered in your sleep." He set his coffee cup down on the counter and started to head for her.

Her throat tightened at those simple words. She never thought she'd have a man like him care about her, even that much. Jay's thoughtfulness touched her in ways she hadn't imagined. As he took the egg carton from her hand, she knew what he had in mind by the hungry glint in his piercing green eyes. And it wasn't breakfast. Turning from her, he set the carton down and before he'd looked back, she stripped off her shirt, shorts and panties and tossed them to the floor in a messy heap.

When he turned to face her, she was just stepping out of her slippers. His big body went still as he drank in the sight of her standing there naked. An undeniable shudder rolled through him as he reached for her. She loved that she still got that reaction out of him. Over a year later and the chemistry was still as powerful as ever.

Sliding her hands up his hard chest, she dug her fingers into his shoulders. Her breasts rubbed against his bare skin, now tingling from the feel of his muscular body instead of the cold.

"You're going to make me late," Jay murmured before hoisting her up so that she had to wrap her legs around his waist. Through his boxers, his erection pressed insistently against her abdomen, making her body flare to life in the way only he could.

"I can head upstairs instead and—"

He cut her off with a scorching kiss that made her toes curl. His big hands cupped her behind as he walked them to the nearest counter and sat her down. When he knelt between her legs, burying his face in her heat, she arched into him with a ragged moan, knowing they were both going to be incredibly late.

And control freak that she was, she still didn't care.

Thirty minutes later, Ellie propped up on one elbow against the kitchen floor and set her chin on Jay's bare chest. "That was amazing," she murmured against his skin, hating that they had to get up soon and head to work.

Looking supremely smug, he grinned at her as he stroked a hand up and down her bare spine. The tile of the kitchen floor was cool beneath them, but she was still coming down from her climax so nothing could dilute her pleasure.

When he groaned and started to sit up she pushed off him and stood. "All right old man, let me help you up."

For a moment, he portrayed such a vulnerable expression that she wanted to smack herself. He was in his late thirties whereas she'd just turned twenty-five—though she felt a hundred some days—and recently he'd made a comment that led her to believe the age difference bothered him a little. Even if it wasn't a big deal to her. Thanks to an apathetic mother and an alcoholic father, she'd grown up with no real childhood to speak of and she'd always felt light years older than she was. With the exception of her deceased sister's help, Ellie had always taken care of herself. "Jay—"

That brief sense of vulnerability she'd seen disappeared as he smiled and stood. He wrapped his big arms around her and brushed his lips over hers, silencing whatever she'd been about to say. "I've gotta head out soon and I'll have to turn my cell to silent for a few hours once I reach the casino."

"Okay. I don't have anything big today. Just joining in two meetings with Wyatt this morning, so if you, want let's meet for lunch. At the Cloud?" What most employees called Cloud 9.

He nodded and kissed her again, this time a claiming that left her breathless. Once he'd gone upstairs she put the eggs up and snagged some coffee. By the time she'd finished it and made her way up to their bedroom, Jay was dressed and looking impossibly sexy in a black suit and silver and green tie she'd bought him. One of his tattoos peeked out on the top of his left hand, part of an intricate script listing the names of friends he'd lost overseas. When she met his gaze again, she saw that familiar hungry look as he watched her.

"Go," she said, close to jumping him again. Then they'd truly be late. "Or we'll both get fired."

He snorted at that. It would take more than that for their boss to fire them. They'd have to burn down the casino for that to happen. "I've got something special planned for tonight, so don't be late getting home."

She paused at the unreadable note in his voice, but nodded. His little surprises were always fun—and always sexy. "It looks like it's going to be a low key kind of week." Of course by saying that she'd probably just cursed herself for a manic one.

Another kiss and he was gone. Moving into gear she showered and was getting dressed when her cell rang. No one called her this early except her boss. Hell, she probably *had* jinxed herself. When she saw the caller ID she frowned, not recognizing the number. But it was local. "Ellie here."

"Eleanor *Johansen*," a familiar, hated voice from her past said with a dripping kind of smugness that made her want to reach through the phone and punch him.

Feeling her blood turn to ice, she collapsed on the edge of the king-sized bed, her knees giving way upon hearing Kevin Murrell on the other end. He wasn't supposed to be out of prison for another fifteen or twenty years. "How'd you get this number?" she demanded, thankful her voice didn't shake. She knew she should just hang up on him, but she needed to find out what this creep wanted. And when he'd gotten out of prison, because she didn't think he could be calling from inside.

He made an obnoxious *tsking* sound. God, how had she ever thought she was in love with this moron? "Taking your mother's maiden name isn't enough to hide from me."

"I'm not trying to hide from anyone." And she wasn't. Not truly. She'd just wanted to put distance between her past self and who she'd become. "I take it you're out. Good behavior?" She couldn't hide a snort of disbelief.

A long pause before he spoke again and this time he didn't hide the bite of annoyance in his voice. "You've changed."

"If you mean I'm different than that pathetic seventeen year old who thought you hung the moon, then yeah, I'm very different. Why are you calling me?" Finding her legs again, she went to her bedroom window and slightly pulled the curtains back. She knew she was likely being paranoid, but she wanted to see if this bastard was watching her house. She wouldn't put it past him. Not when she had something he wanted.

"You know why. I want my belongings."

Ice settled into a hard ball in her stomach as she had to confess the truth. "I've got most of it, but I don't have all of it."

Another pause, longer this time. "How short am I?"

She closed her eyes, rubbing her temple. "About fifty." Meaning fifty thousand dollars. For all she knew he was being monitored by the police or even the criminal he'd stolen from in the first place. "I didn't expect you to get out for a few more years." Because she would have replaced the money by then, with him none the wiser. She wasn't sorry she'd taken it, not when it had given her a path to college and a better life. Kevin had stolen half a million from a low level mobster before getting arrested for something completely unrelated. Since Nevada was a three-strike state and he'd committed his third felony robbery of a residence with a deadly weapon, he'd been locked up and was supposed to have been kept there for a good long time. Looked like the justice system failed again.

He was silent again, but this time when he spoke she could practically hear the glee in his voice. "No bother then, you can return what you've still got and do me one little favor. Then we'll call it even."

She swallowed hard, knowing his type of 'favor' wasn't something she'd be willing to do. Especially not if it was worth fifty thousand to him. She was tempted to hang up on Kevin, but knew it would be a mistake. He'd just harass her in person. "Favor?"

"You're going to help me rob the Serafina. And if you don't, I'm going to rip apart the pretty little life you've made for yourself. I'll start by telling De Luca you stole his money."

Without responding she ended the call, fighting the panic bubbling up inside her. She wasn't sure if Carlo De Luca would actually believe she'd taken his money, but she couldn't take the chance he would and come after those she loved.

Fighting panic, she went to her closet and grabbed a small suitcase. Staying here like a sitting duck wasn't the answer. Her phone rang again, but she ignored it as she started grabbing clothes from the closet she shared with Jay. For a brief moment she thought of confessing everything to him, but knew she couldn't. Because he'd want to go all protector male on her and the type of people Kevin associated with didn't play by any rules.

They were true criminals who had no problem killing others to get what they wanted. She couldn't drag Jay into that. She loved him too much. Plus, deep down, she knew that her sweet, perfect Jay wouldn't understand the decisions she'd made at seventeen. She'd had obstacles she refused to let stand in her way and had made some hard decisions that she didn't regret. But Jay hadn't grown up like that and he wouldn't get it.

He'd judge her, look at her differently and in the end, he'd cut ties with her anyway. No, she'd have to cut and run to keep him safe and to keep her own secrets safe. She'd leave him a note and once she'd figured out this mess and put some distance between her and Kevin, she'd call Jay to let him know she was okay. Until then, she couldn't pull him into the gutter with her. He didn't deserve it and she'd never put him in danger. This is what she got for thinking she could actually be happy.

CHAPTER TWO

Ellie smoothed a hand down her black pencil skirt as she handed her boss Wyatt his planner with detailed notes about his meetings and other agendas for the next month. She had three different alerts sent to his phone for meetings, but he was old school and liked to have a physical reminder on hand. Probably because he'd learned to tune out the alerts. "Remember, the meeting next Tuesday is very important, Wyatt. You've put it off twice already and—"

"I won't miss it," he said, taking his planner and setting it down without looking at it. He stared at his laptop, his fingers clacking away on the keys as he spoke. "Besides, you're coming with me to that one. I don't know why you're so stressed today."

She bit her lip, trying to find the right words. Impossible ones she just needed to get out. Maybe the silence was more weighted than she realized because he looked up then, his blue eyes electric in their intensity.

"You are going with me to that meeting?"

"Wyatt, I've enjoyed working for you more than I can say." She smoothed her hand down her skirt again, a stupid nervous habit.

His expression went flat. "You're not quitting."

She blinked at his forceful tone. "I appreciate everything you did for me when I graduated." He'd given her a job right out of school. She'd just gotten her Master's in Business Administration and had been hungry to work. Landing a position with one of the richest men in the country had been a dream come true. She worked her ass off, but he compensated all his employees well and she loved what she did. Leaving this position was one of the hardest decisions, but she knew she had to do it. Once she told Kevin that she'd been fired—a tiny lie—she wouldn't be able to help him with whatever plan he had to rob the Serafina. This was the only way.

Frowning, Wyatt stood, pushing his chair back before rounding his desk. Wearing a custom-made pin-striped suit, the tall man with midnight black hair and electric blue eyes, that were so damn intense as to be scary, was giving her all his focus. She didn't like feeling as if she were under a microscope, but stood her ground.

Crossing his arms over his chest, he leaned against the front of his desk and faced off with her. Even though he wasn't as tall as Jay, the man was certainly intimidating. She'd seen him use this glare with business associates and even enemies before and had never thought to be on the receiving end of one of his 'looks'. "Are you giving your resignation?" he asked quietly, disbelief threading through every word.

Even though she wanted to stay strong, she dropped her gaze and fished out the folded piece of paper she'd tucked in the back of her skirt. It was slightly wrinkled as she handed it to him. "I'm sorry that I can't give you two weeks' notice and if you won't give me a reference I completely understand. I hope that you will as I've enjoyed working here, but—"

"I'm not accepting your resignation," he said calmly, his bluntness taking her by surprise. She forced herself to meet his gaze again. "Is this about you and Jay? Are you guys having problems? Whatever this is about, we'll work it out. Do you want a raise? Hell, you deserve one so consider it done, effective tomorrow."

She shook her head, taken aback by the offer. "I..." For a brief moment she thought of telling him that her thieving ex-boyfriend wanted her to steal from him. If she didn't work here anymore, the bastard couldn't blackmail her into anything. Which meant she'd become useless to Kevin and he'd leave her alone. She knew how that rat Kevin operated. But if she stayed on as Wyatt's assistant, she'd *always* be a target for Kevin. He would keep coming at her until someone in her life got hurt. Even if she paid him back all 'his' money—which she planned to scrounge together in the next couple days—he'd never leave her alone and she refused to steal from the people she'd come to care for. Even if it meant leaving the man she loved and starting over somewhere new, she had to do it. She couldn't drag good people into her mess, especially not if Kevin got Carlo De Luca involved. That had *absolute nightmare* written all over it. "This has nothing to do with Jay. I'm leaving for personal reasons."

Wyatt set the resignation letter on the desk and eyed her carefully, assessing her. As if he could read her mind. "Are you in trouble? Is this about money?" Before she could answer, he rounded the desk and pulled out a leather pouch from his top right hand drawer where she knew he kept his petty cash.

He pulled out a wad of bills and held it out. "There's three thousand dollars here, but I can get more quickly. All I've gotta do is go downstairs. What's going on?"

She stared at the money and quickly computed what she needed to do to get the rest of the cash for her ex. Most of her money was tied up in investments and her retirement fund, but she had about thirty-five thousand in savings. She could sell her car, which should get her another five thousand—but she needed it. Selling it wouldn't be smart. Still, she had some nice jewelry that might net her another five thousand. If she sold her car and took Wyatt's three she'd only have two to go... But she simply couldn't take it. No, she could borrow the last bit from an old acquaintance. The interest would be high but she wouldn't be taking from someone like Wyatt. He was a good boss and a good man. Just…no. She couldn't do it.

Stepping back, she put some distance between them before the temptation grew to be too much. She'd got herself into this mess, she'd get herself out. "Thank you, but no. I really am sorry about this. I'll get my things later."

"I'm not accepting this resignation." As if to prove it, he ripped the paper into bits. "Deal with whatever you need to, but you still have a place here. Always."

Her throat tightened as tears choked her, making it impossible to speak. Horrified that she was about to break down and confess everything, she turned and fled the office, batting away the wetness on her cheeks. She had some belongings in her office that she'd need to get, but couldn't do it now. She'd send for everything later. Deep down she worried about her decision, but if she told Wyatt and Jay everything she knew *exactly* what would happen.

They'd attempt to protect her and she couldn't let that happen. Because men like Kevin and De Luca fought dirty and violently. Jay and Wyatt might be trained, but they were *good* men who walked on the right side of the law. She couldn't make Jay a walking target because of her. The thought of him or anyone else she cared about getting caught in the crossfire because of her stupid youthful mistakes clawed at her. She simply couldn't have that hanging over her head. If anything happened to Jay it would destroy her. The only thing that semi eased her conscience was the fact that she would call him as soon as she'd made it safely out of town. She didn't want him to worry, but a little worry was better than him ending up dead. And if he didn't know where she was, he was useless to Kevin too.

As Ellie raced from his office, Wyatt immediately dialed Jay. When his friend and personal bodyguard didn't answer, he cursed. Of course he wasn't going to pick up. Jay was conducting interviews all morning. Whatever was going on with Ellie, Wyatt was going to get to the bottom of it. He couldn't believe that Jay would let Ellie just walk in here and blindside him like this. The man was the head of his personal security, but they were also friends. Which meant Ellie hadn't told Jay she was quitting either.

Wyatt had seen the way she watched the cash he'd tried to give her. Something had her running scared and there was no way in hell he was letting her take care of it herself. He didn't care for many people, but she was one of the few. She put up with his sometimes tyrannical attitude, as his wife Iris liked to call it, and was one of the hardest workers he'd ever had. Not to mention she'd made Jay happier than Wyatt had ever thought possible.

And Jay was more than just a friend or employee. The man was family. By extension, so was Ellie.

As he grabbed his jacket from behind his chair, he dialed Nicholas Brannon, another one of his personal security members who also worked at the Serafina when Wyatt was in town—which lately was more and more often. Normally he'd call Iris or Hayden, but he knew they were doing security drills with the newest employees.

"Hey, boss," Brannon answered on the first ring.

"Where are you?" There wasn't time to bother with niceties.

"By one of the east exits near the blackjack tables. Hayden saw some suspicious activities on one of the live feeds and told me—"

"Whatever it is, someone else can take care of it. Head to the west side elevators near the marble fountain with the mermaid sculpture. Ellie should be exiting very soon. I want you to tail her. Grab one of the unused company vehicles from valet if you can't get to yours."

"On my way... Is this Jay's Ellie we're talking about?" he asked, even as Wyatt heard him moving into action as he likely ran toward the elevators.

"Yeah. Stay unseen, but whatever you do, do *not* lose her. And keep her safe."

Brannon snorted as if that was a given. "No problem. How often should I check in?"

"Once you're on the road call me and we'll leave the line open. I've gotta make a couple other calls first." He had to get hold of Jay, but he wasn't telling Brannon that.

"All right, I'll make sure she's okay."

"Thanks." Wyatt was glad the other man didn't question him. Not that he'd expected Brannon to.

Just like Wyatt, the man was also a former Marine. He'd been Force Recon and had spent a lot of time behind enemy lines. He was good at getting into places unseen. If anyone could tail Ellie without her knowledge, it was Brannon. Because Ellie was sharp and unlike most people, she would notice someone following her. She might not be physically tough or trained like Iris, but the woman was a fighter and very aware of her surroundings at all times. Something he'd noticed about her the first day they'd met. It was one of the reasons he'd hired her. She'd been qualified, sure, but she'd also been completely untried in the real world. Still, she'd been a lot more than a pretty face and he'd recognized something in her he saw in himself. A hunger to succeed. He knew enough about her past that he understood why. He did detailed background checks on everyone who worked with him.

Once he reached one of his private elevators, he put in his master key card and headed to one of the employee parking lots where he could choose from a multitude of company vehicles. He wasn't driving his own SUV right now in case Ellie noticed him.

Brannon called him ten minutes later and gave him a general location. "She just turned on Tropicana. If she hits 515, I might lose her."

Wyatt gritted his teeth and took a sharp turn at the next intersection. He'd been trying Jay, but the man still wasn't answering. Probably because he'd turned his phone to silent. "If you want to keep your job, you won't lose her." He knew he was being irrational because the truth was if Ellie got on the so-called Spaghetti Bowl, the aptly named Las Vegas freeway, it would be damn hard to stay with her.

"Damn, boss," Brannon muttered.

Wyatt ignored the other man as he tried to push down the concern rising inside him. "Where are you now?"

"Hold on...she's turning." When Brannon rattled off a familiar street, Wyatt frowned.

There was nothing down there but pawn stores, gun shops and strip clubs. Before he could ask what she was doing, Brannon said, "She's pulling into the parking lot of Ultimate Pawn. I'm going to stop next door at The Gold Mine Pawn."

"All right, see you in a couple minutes." After they disconnected he made the decision and called Iris. The more he thought about Ellie's behavior, the more he realized something was truly off and he was going to use all his resources to help her.

His wife, who was also the head of security at the Serafina, answered on the second ring. "Hey, babe." He could hear the steady thrum of voices in the background, telling him she was in the security room.

"Hey, have you or Hayden heard from Jay this morning?"

"I talked to him a couple hours ago before he started all those interviews." Her tone went from relaxed to battle-mode in a second. "He was in here about twenty minutes ago telling me he was taking a break in between interviewees. He had to run home for something. What's wrong?"

"Ellie just quit and now she's pulling into a pawn shop."

"What... hold on." Seconds later, the background noise was eliminated so he knew Iris was in her office out of hearing range of anyone else. He could see his tall, slender, and incredibly fierce wife leaning against the custom made desk she rarely used, frowning. "Jay was going to propose tonight. Hayden told me this morning because he couldn't keep it a secret any longer. Jay didn't seem upset when he stopped by, but do you think that's why she quit?"

"No." His answer was instant. "I think she's scared of something. Or needs money for something."

"Did you offer her help or...never mind, of course you did. What do you need from me?"

"Get V to work his magic and track her phone. She's at a pawn shop right now but I don't know where she's going next."

V was short for Vadim, a man they'd both served with during their time in the Marines. Oddly enough, not at the same time. Though Wyatt and Iris had both been in the Marines at the same time—though she'd been in longer than him—they'd never done any missions together or been stationed anywhere together that he knew of. Somehow they both knew Vadim and when Wyatt had invited his old friend over for dinner two months ago—in an attempt to hire him—it had been a surprise to V, Iris and Wyatt that they were all acquainted. Thankfully his old friend had taken the job because the man was a genius when it came to computers. Now Wyatt desperately needed that expertise to help someone they all considered family.

And he still needed to get in touch with Jay. But he wasn't leaving Brannon to follow Ellie on his own.

CHAPTER THREE

*I'm ready to move on. Please don't search for me.
Please just let me go.*

Jay tried to wrap his mind around the insane letter from Ellie he'd just finished reading. It went on to say that she'd had fun with him but was done with their relationship and her time in Vegas and she'd get the rest of her stuff later. What. The. Hell?

Slamming it down onto his kitchen table, he forced himself to take a deep breath and tried to think rationally. Whatever had brought on this note, it wasn't because she didn't love him. He *knew* Ellie. She might have kept a part of herself separate from him and the rest of the world, but he knew her better than anyone.

And there was no way in hell he'd let her go.

He pulled his cell from his pants' pocket and cursed when he realized he hadn't turned the ringer back on. He'd had a space of time in between interviewees and needed to run home before he met Ellie for lunch. With half a dozen missed calls from Wyatt, a lead ball congealed in his stomach. If she was truly done with her time in Vegas… He hadn't even been thinking about her job. As Jay raced up the stairs, he dialed his boss.

"Where are you?" Wyatt asked, his tone tense.

"Home." He paused as he took in the bedroom he shared with Ellie. Her soft touches were everywhere, from the four poster bed with the gauzy canopy draped over it that she'd declared *wasn't* too girly because of its simplistic style. Whatever that meant. It was frilly and if any of his buddies from the Teams could see what he slept in they'd give him so much grief—and he didn't care because it made Ellie happy. He'd made love to her there too many times to count. The thought of crawling into it without her made him feel hollow inside.

"Ellie quit. You know anything about that?" His boss spoke cautiously, as if he didn't want to anger a rabid bear.

Which is what Jay felt like at the moment. His throat tightened as Wyatt's words registered. As the reality of what was actually happening settled into his bones, slicing at him with no reprieve. "She left a note. Ending things. I just found it." He barely rasped the words out as he went straight for their closet. Most of her stuff was there, but one of her bags was gone and he could tell certain clothes and shoes were missing.

"What the hell's going on?"

"I don't know." But he had to find her. Now. "Things have been great between us. This morning we…" He trailed off, not wanting to finish that sentence. He'd planned to propose to her tonight, and she'd taken off. Deep down he wondered if maybe she'd somehow found out and that was why she'd left. Racing back downstairs, he said, "We've gotta find her. Ask V to—"

"Already on it. He's tracking her phone as we speak. Brannon and I followed her to a pawn shop. I went in after she left and Brannon is tailing her now. She sold some nice jewelry, Jay. Including earrings I know were a gift from her grandmother."

Hearing that was like a punch straight to the face, swift and sharp. Ellie would never sell those diamonds. Not unless something was seriously wrong. Heart pounding fast as he headed to the garage, he found his voice. "We've got to find her. Whatever's going on is bad. She wouldn't just leave like this unless she was scared." And Jay was going to figure out what the hell had scared the woman he loved enough to bolt like this. Because this had come out of nowhere. If something had been bothering her, he'd have known, so whatever this was about, something had very recently scared her.

"I know. I bought the earrings back."

Relief slid through him even though that was the least of his worries. "What's your location?"

After Wyatt rattled off a familiar street that would take Jay a solid twenty minutes to get to if he took a shortcut, he said, "Brannon's calling. I'll call or text with our next stop."

"Don't lose her," Jay ordered, not caring that Wyatt was his boss.

"We won't."

As they disconnected, Jay slid into his truck and gunned the engine. He called Ellie twice, but each time it went straight to voicemail. Not exactly a surprise considering that note and the fact that she'd quit her job. Emotions battled inside him. He was scared for Ellie, but he couldn't shove back the anger that she'd just up and left like this. Before he'd made it to the end of his street his phone pinged with an incoming text. He read the message from Wyatt and froze.

Ellie had just parked at one of the sleaziest strip clubs in Vegas. And had gone inside using one of the side doors. Alone. Of her own free will. Fighting panic and a big dose of anger that she hadn't trusted him with whatever the hell was going on, Jay took a sharp left and broke too many traffic laws to think about as he made his way to a shady part of town Ellie had no business being in. He was going to get his damn answers and help her whether she wanted it or not.

This was the last place on earth Ellie wanted to be, but the owner of Teaser's, a low rent strip club in a seedy part of town, might lend her the money she needed. She'd realized she couldn't sell her car and would need a bigger chunk of cash since her jewelry hadn't sold for as much as she'd thought it would. Considering it was practically rolling off her in waves, the owner of the pawn shop had likely sensed her desperation. It sliced deep that she'd had to sell her grandmother's earrings, but if she could get Kevin out of her life forever, it was a price she was willing to pay.

She couldn't even think about what Jay's reaction would be when he found her note—or if Wyatt got to him first. Because she wasn't stupid enough to think Wyatt wouldn't tell Jay. Tears burned her eyes at the thought of Jay's pain, but she brushed them away and ruthlessly shoved down her guilt and agony.

Instead of using the main entrance, she headed around the side of the building toward the back. She'd been here years ago with Kevin when he'd done a couple shady deals and had used the club as a distraction/cover for said deals. She still couldn't believe what an idiot seventeen year old she'd been and how she'd ever thought he was anything special. Now she realized how lucky she'd been to come out of that relationship unscathed.

It had been a dark time in her life, especially after her sister's death, but it still disgusted her that she'd ever thought Kevin was boyfriend material. He was barely human being material.

She glanced up at the video camera in the right upper hand corner above the door. Kevin had confided to her that the thing was fake and it still looked as if it was the same one. Which was probably why there was a peephole in the door. Bracing herself for the no doubt uncomfortable conversation she was about to face, she rapped her knuckles against the door.

Seconds later it opened and she blinked in surprise. Cody Hurley, a boy she'd gone to high school with stood there wearing dark slacks and a black, long-sleeved shirt with a small security emblem over his left pec. He looked just as surprised as she felt.

"Ellie, what are you doing here?" He looked around the alleyway before stepping back so she could come inside.

The hallway smelled like cheap perfume and cigarettes. Further past the hallway she could feel as well as hear the steady, rattling thump of music. "Hey, Cody, you work here?" It was hard to keep the surprise out of her voice. He'd been a star football player and had received a full scholarship to college because of his talent. Now he was working at Teaser's?

His jaw tightened as he nodded. "Yeah, lost my scholarship and got into some trouble. Did a short stint in prison and this was the only job I could get. The only legal job," he added.

Her eyes widened as she tried to think of something polite to say. She wasn't sure how to respond to a revelation like that. "I'm...sorry. You were so talented. That's a tough break."

He gave her a short nod, then glanced over his shoulder before focusing on her. "What the hell are you doing here? This isn't a place for someone like you," he said quietly. "I heard you got a really good job with Wyatt Christiansen. You're not...looking for work *here* are you?"

She shook her head, embarrassed by the thought. "No, but I need to talk to Leonard, if he still owns the place." Something she probably should have looked up, but she'd been so manic in her need to get cash together fast she hadn't been thinking everything through.

"He does."

She raised her eyebrows when he didn't elaborate. "Well, is he here?" She wrapped her arms around herself when Cody simply stood there, his expression remote and his body like a barrier to the rest of the hallway. As if he wasn't going to let her pass.

"Yeah, but Ellie, he's no good. Whatever you're looking for, find it somewhere else. This is not—"

At the sound of a door opening, Cody stopped talking and turned around. Ellie peered around his broad body and saw Leonard stepping out from what she assumed was his office. With brown hair he'd teased to look bigger—and likely covered with hairspray to get that ridiculous helmet style—and a white T-shirt under his seventies-style jacket and a big gold chain, he looked exactly like the man she remembered. Tacky.

He recognized her immediately, if the lecherous grin on his face was any indication. Or maybe that was the way he looked at all females. Whatever. She just needed to borrow money and he would be a hell of a lot easier to borrow from than one of those places that would require paperwork and personal information.

"Ellie Wickliff," he said, even his voice having an oily quality that made her stomach turn.

Her last name was now Johansen since she'd taken her mother's maiden name, but she didn't correct him. It was creepy enough that he remembered her last name. She nodded and stepped around Cody. "Good to see you again," she murmured, before striding toward Leonard. "You have a few minutes?"

He nodded and held out a hand to the room he'd just stepped from. "Anything for you."

Ugh, gross. She faltered once, rethinking her decision. But she needed that money. She could push her way through an uncomfortable conversation. She thought she heard Cody mutter a curse behind her as Leonard shut the door to his office. At least he didn't attempt to lock it.

As he moved to the other side of his desk, some of her tension faded and she didn't feel quite so caged. "You here for a job?" he asked as he raked a gaze over her body.

It didn't matter that she was completely clothed, the man made her feel exposed with that look. She wanted to cross her arms over her chest, but resisted the instinct. She couldn't let him see that he bothered her. "No, but I know you lend money. I need ten thousand and I can pay it back within four weeks." Since she wasn't selling her car and she hadn't been able to get as much for her earrings as she'd hoped, she'd known that guy at the pawn would give her the same crappy deal on her diamond bracelet. She didn't think she'd need the full ten thousand, but wanted a little buffer of funds. Before Leonard could answer, she pulled the bracelet from the side pocket of her purse. "This was six thousand, but you could probably sell it for half that. I'll give you this as collateral and collect once I've paid you back everything."

His eyebrows rose as he shifted in his seat, his chair creaking. "Ten thousand is a lot."

She nearly snorted. He probably had triple that in one of his safes. And thanks to Kevin, she knew Leonard had multiple safes here. She didn't respond though, just waited for him to continue since he hadn't asked a question.

"What do you need it for?"

"Why does it matter? Either you'll lend it to me or you won't." She knew she couldn't act too desperate or he'd pounce. Of course the fact that she was here made it clear she needed the funds in a bad way.

His eyes held a speculative gleam. "How do I know you're good for it?"

She set the bracelet on the desk, then pulled out a copy of one of her retirement funds. She'd blacked out her account information and her address, but her name was still visible. Sliding it across the desk, she said, "I've got the money, but it's not liquid right now. I need a couple weeks to withdraw the funds and for them to send me a check. It might not take that long, but it'll be at least a week." They made taking money out of retirement funds early hard for a reason. You weren't supposed to do it.

He let out a low whistle. "You certainly are good for it. Tell you what." He looked up, pinning her with that jarring gaze that made her want to wrap up in a thick robe so he couldn't see an inch of her. "You give me a private dance, right here, right now, and I'll give you the cash. Three-point-five percent interest too."

She blinked at his words, grossed out by the dance request and stunned by the percentage. That was incredibly low for a loan shark, a bank, or anyone lending money. It didn't make sense for him to offer it. "I'm not going to dance for you."

He shrugged and lifted his arms, setting his hands behind his head as he leaned back. "Why not? I'm not going to touch you and you'll never get that interest rate anywhere else." He sounded smug, as if he already assumed she'd say yes.

Desperate or not, she wasn't taking off her damn clothes for anyone. She snagged her bracelet from the desk and shoved it in her purse. "No thanks." Since there was no more to say, she turned for the door. She'd get the money another way.

As her hand touched the doorknob, a sharp tug on her hair made her cry out. Her eyes watered as her head jerked back under the force of Leonard's grip.

"You always thought you were better than everyone," he snarled as he slung her to the floor by her hair. She fell to her knees, pain shooting through them as they slammed against the hardwood.

She reached up and struggled to dislodge his hand from her hair when he kicked her in the ribs. She screamed from the shooting agony and instinctively went to grip her side when he ripped open the front of her blouse with a vicious tug.

Iciness slammed through her as she realized his intent. At the same time, her position on the floor registered and she hauled back and punched him between the legs.

"Bitch!" Crying out, he let go of her hair as he doubled over. Holding onto her purse, she jumped to her feet, ready to clock him across the head with it when the door flew open.

Cody stood there, taking in the scene with a grim expression.

"Shut and lock that door," Leonard wheezed out as she managed to stand. "You're going to help me teach this bitch a lesson or you're fired."

Terror punched through Ellie as she looked between the man blocking her getaway and the one she'd just punched in the nuts.

CHAPTER FOUR

Jay felt as if he was running on autopilot as he pushed open one of the darkly tinted glass doors of Teaser's strip club. There was a small entryway with a scantily dressed woman sitting behind a cash register. She wore a see-through black lace bra and a plaid skirt the size of a band-aid. Her legs were crossed, a bored expression on her face until she saw him. Her eyes lit up as she looked him over with a lustful gaze. Before he could say anything she nodded toward the doorway covered by sparkly hanging beads. "No charge, honey." Despite her likely being in her early twenties, her voice was raspy like a decade's-long smoker.

He nodded politely, his body disrupting the beads with a noisy jangle as he stepped into a darker room with a steady thump of rock filtering through the place. A half-naked woman was on one of the five stages dressed in a school girl outfit while Cherry Pie blared. Ignoring the sight the dozen or so men closest to the stage were glued to, he scanned the place until he saw Wyatt and Brannon talking to another scantily dressed woman. Who was also wearing one of those plaid school girl skirts. Maybe it was a theme today.

Jay hurried over and realized the woman was holding a drink tray as she leaned against the only bar that appeared to be in use. Sidestepping a woman who asked if he wanted a private dance, he nodded once at Wyatt when the other man spotted him. All he cared about was finding Ellie and making sure she was okay.

Breaking away from Brannon and the female, Wyatt met him halfway, about ten feet away from the other two. They wouldn't have been able to overhear him and Wyatt with the music anyway. "Where's Ellie?" Jay asked.

"Not sure. She went in the side door and we haven't seen her anywhere in here, but she didn't leave. Brannon knows that dancer," he said with a tilt of his head. "She says the owner isn't exactly a loan shark, but he lends money sometimes to locals. His office is in the back so she might be—"

Jay didn't wait for Wyatt to continue. He turned and threaded his way through the mostly empty cocktail tables. As he moved, he catalogued how many people were by the live stage, the bar and the few stragglers sitting at random tables. He also noted the exits, something he did everywhere he went. It was akin to breathing. Three were visible, but he knew there had to be more. Behind him he thought he heard Wyatt mutter something under his breath, but ignored him as he entered the hallway. The music was still audible here, but at a much lower decibel.

His heart rate picked up a notch when he heard a male shout and Ellie's scream from the only door cracked open in the hall. That sound was like a knife to his chest. Withdrawing his SIG, he slowed as he reached the edge of the opening. He risked a quick glance behind him, unsurprised to find Wyatt had also drawn a weapon.

Even though he wanted to blast his way in there, Jay used his training and common sense to slowly ease the door open with his boot. He could see Ellie's purse on the floor turned on its side. Beads of sweat dotted his forehead as he held up a hand motioning to Wyatt that he was going in and that Wyatt should hold off. He knew Wyatt would understand why.

He was basically going in blind and needed backup in case things went south.

"Stop!" Ellie screamed.

The sound of Ellie's terror slammed into Jay. He slammed his foot into the door, deciding to use the element of surprise as he swept the room with his weapon. It took scant seconds to assess the situation.

A big man wearing all black had a smaller man pinned against the wall, his hand wrapped around the guy's throat as he gasped for breath. The smaller man looked like an extra out of a seventies' porno, but Jay's focus was on Ellie. Tears streamed down her face and her silk blouse was ripped right down the middle, exposing her soft skin and lacy bra.

Her expression was terrified as she pointed at the big man. "Jay, he saved me! Don't let him kill that bastard and throw his life away."

The big man looked over his shoulder, a murderous expression on his face as he glanced at Jay and now Wyatt, who Jay could hear entering behind him. Still holding the smaller man against the wall, the man who'd saved Ellie blinked, as if coming out of a daze. He still didn't let go, but he loosened his grip a fraction so the other man could drag in a couple breaths.

The most profound sense of relief slammed into Jay at seeing her unharmed. It was like a body blow. "Ellie, what's going on?" he asked, putting himself between her and the two strangers.

"I..." To Jay's utter surprise she burst into tears, real sobs wrenching from her in a way he'd never imagined. Ellie never cried. Not even when they were arguing—which wasn't very often. She'd once told him she'd rather punch him to make him see the error of his ways than to use tears to her advantage.

Though he wanted to comfort her, Jay wasn't lowering his weapon. He held it steady on the other two men.

The man in the dark clothing looked past Jay and for a moment he saw a flash of recognition in those brown eyes as he focused on Wyatt. Just as quickly, the man looked at Jay. "My name is Cody and I work—worked—here as security. I found Leonard here attacking Ellie and decided to beat the shit out of him."

Jay flicked a glance at Ellie for confirmation. She wasn't crying anymore, just sniffling as she held the pieces of her shirt closed over her chest. She nodded in affirmation, her eyes wide and glassy with the remnants of lingering unshed tears. Immediately he sheathed his weapon in his concealed shoulder holster, mainly because he knew Wyatt was backing him up, and crossed the few feet to Ellie.

To his surprise, she ran into his arms and wrapped her arms around his waist as she buried her face against his chest. Holding her close, he inhaled her subtle vanilla scent as she trembled in his arms. She was usually so feisty and outspoken he sometimes forgot how petite she truly was. At barely five feet, two inches, she seemed almost fragile as he held her.

He rubbed a gentle hand up and down her spine, murmuring soothing words to her while keeping an eye on the other two men. Despite his anger at her, a primal protectiveness swelled inside him, making him pull her closer. Wyatt had come up next to him, weapon not pointed at the men, but held firmly in his hand.

While Jay had a dozen questions, he knew he needed to comfort Ellie first. Even though he wanted to get her the hell out of there, she needed to be calmer first. When she finally pulled back, mascara smudged under her eyes as she looked up at him with embarrassment. "I'm sorry."

He ignored the apology for now. They had a ton to talk about, but not with an audience. "Did he *hurt* you?" The inflection in his voice made it clear what type of hurt he meant.

Ellie shook her head. "Not like that. He pulled my hair, threw me to the ground and kicked me in the ribs, but Cody—"

Jay swiveled to face Leonard, using his body to block Ellie's. For a moment, a red haze rimmed his vision. Maybe he should have let Cody beat the shit out of this guy. When Jay felt Wyatt's hand on his chest pushing back, his blue eyes filled with silent warning, Jay froze. He hadn't even realized he'd taken a step toward Leonard. And if Wyatt hadn't stopped him, he knew he'd have done something he couldn't take back.

He narrowed his gaze on the red-faced man still pinned to the wall. Cody had let the guy slide down so that he was on his feet and had given him enough space that he could breathe properly. "Ellie, do you want to press charges?" Jay needed to know if they should call the police and since he didn't have all the details of why Ellie was even here, he wasn't sure what the hell she'd want to do.

"No."

"Wyatt..." Jay trailed off as he stepped forward, knowing his friend would protect Ellie if need be. Stalking closer to Cody, he said, "Drop him."

The security guy didn't pause, just let his arm drop and stepped away as Jay zeroed in on Leonard.

After a quick pat down told him the guy wasn't armed, Jay stood, towering over the man as he glared at him. Very soon Jay was going to find out everything possible about this piece of garbage who had dared to touch his Ellie. And he was going to make Leonard regret it. "Give me your wallet."

Despite the terror oozing off him, the man blinked, as if that was the last thing he'd expected Jay to say. "What?"

Jay rammed his fist into the man's ribs, a sense of pure elation humming through him as Leonard doubled over, crying out in pain. Holding onto his side, he held up one hand in surrender before reaching into his back pocket. Still wheezing, he pulled out his wallet and held it up with shaking fingers.

Jay opened it and took the man's driver's license out, making sure Leonard Smith—Smith, really?—saw him do it before he tossed the wallet to the hardwood floor. Then he shoved the license into his own pocket. Leaning close so that only the man could hear him, Jay whispered menacingly. "You come near Ellie again, even think about her, I'll gut you and leave you in the desert for the coyotes to feed on. I'll watch as they rip your flesh apart. Ellie does not exist to you. Understand?"

Eyes wide with raw fear, the man nodded as he straightened, wincing in obvious pain.

Jay wasn't sure if he believed the guy so he'd be following up. Stepping back, he put some distance between them, but still didn't take his eyes off the bastard. Once he'd reached Ellie and Wyatt, he saw that Ellie was wearing Wyatt's jacket to help her cover up. She clutched her purse to her chest as if it could protect her. And she was shaking. Shit. He needed to get her out of there.

Questions later, he reminded himself. Wrapping his arm around Ellie's shoulders, he started to steer her out of the room when he saw Brannon hovering in the hallway acting as a lookout. He nodded once to indicate they were clear, but before they could leave, Ellie stopped and swiveled in the direction of the security guy.

"Cody, are you going to be okay? I'm sorry I got you fired." The words spilled from her at once as if she'd just found her voice again.

"This was a long time coming." There was a dark, deadly edge to the man's voice that surprised Jay. "You guys get out of here. I'm going to clean up this mess."

Unsure exactly what the guy meant, and not really caring, Jay squeezed Ellie's shoulders. "Come on."

"We can go out this way," she said quietly, motioning toward the end of the hall in the opposite direction of the pulsing beat of the club.

After checking the alleyway, they all spilled out into the bright sunlight. The glare was jarring after being in the darker atmosphere, but Jay didn't release his grip on Ellie.

"Wyatt, Brannon." He nodded at them, indicating they should walk ahead. He wanted them gone so he could talk to Ellie alone.

She still wouldn't look at him, was looking anywhere but at him in fact. Currently her gaze was on her shoes, three-inch heels that she'd worn once before while they'd made love on the counter in their kitchen. He quickly shoved that thought away.

As the other two men moved toward the parking lot, Jay turned Ellie so that she had to face him. Now that she was safe and he was able to touch her, the anger burning inside him pushed toward the surface. "We talk here or at home. Your choice."

"Jay..."

"No," he said savagely. "I come home on a break to find a bullshit note from you, throwing away our relationship like it meant nothing, then I find out from Wyatt that you quit with no notice. You're going to talk about whatever the hell scared you enough to run. So you get a choice. Here. Or home."

Shifting from one foot to the other and still not looking at him, she finally whispered, "Home."

"So your girl is in?" Carlo De Luca spoke in that soft, almost monotone voice, his hawk-like gaze pinned on Kevin.

De Luca wore a three piece suit, everything no doubt custom made. The man ran one of the biggest criminal enterprises in Vegas and clearly accepted only the best of everything. The property Kevin stood in now was proof enough of that. He actually hadn't been allowed inside the mansion, but had been escorted around the side of De Luca's home until they reached a massive, glistening pool and patio area. A couple half-naked women were sunbathing, but no one paid them any attention.

Kevin tried not to squirm under that stare. He was in this mess because of his own big mouth and now he'd have to come through. When he'd heard Ellie was working for one of the richest men in Vegas—hell, probably the country—he'd thought she'd have no problem helping him out.

In his experience people didn't change who they were. She might not have gone in on any heists with him, but she'd driven the getaway car once. Of course, she hadn't known about it until afterward, but still, the bitch had known what type of man he was and she'd been fine with it. He just needed to see Ellie in person and convince her to help him—and give him his money. Technically it was De Luca's and if the man had any inkling that Kevin had stolen from him, he'd be wrapped up in tires right now and burning in the middle of the desert. Fortunately De Luca had no clue that the man who'd stolen his five hundred Gs was sitting on his spotless patio.

Kevin cleared his throat and nodded. "Yeah, she'll be in."

"She will be or she *is* in?" That gaze narrowed again and his voice took on just the slightest inflection. De Luca still spoke low, but something about that tone put Kevin on edge.

Damn, he needed to keep it together. It was just nerves, that was all. He'd been in prison for almost eight years and everything was an adjustment now. Meeting one of De Luca's men on the inside had been stupid luck. Unlike some dumbasses who bragged about their crimes, Kevin kept his business to himself. All these years he'd never told a soul he'd stolen from De Luca. The others who'd helped him pull off the heist were all dead—because he'd put a bullet in each of their heads. Something Ellie had no clue about. She'd started to pull away from him right before he got pinched that third time so he'd started keeping stuff from her. Not because he'd worried she'd narc on him, but because he hadn't wanted to scare her off. He was actually surprised she'd kept it—most of it—especially since she'd never come to see him. She'd taken a couple of his collect calls, but that was it. Then she'd gone to college and cut contact completely. "Yeah, she's in. No doubt. We go way back, she won't let me down." He wouldn't let her. If he had to force her to help, he'd do it.

De Luca flicked a glance over Kevin's shoulder and made a subtle gesture with his hand. A moment later, Kevin felt a strong hand on his shoulder. Looking up he found one of De Luca's nameless men staring at him. He jerked his chin toward the side of the house. "Time to go."

Nodding, Kevin stood. "Thanks for meeting with me, Mr. De Luca." The mobster wasn't even paying attention to him as one of the half-naked women who'd been swimming in his pool now perched on his lap, giggling at something the man said.

Gritting his teeth, struggling not to show his annoyance, Kevin followed the thug around the side of the house. One day he'd own something exactly like this. Hell, maybe he'd own this very property. De Luca's man escorted Kevin to his car without a word. Seconds after he'd driven off the property, the iron gate blocking off the driveway shut behind him. A moment after that, his phone rang.

When he saw Tadeo's number on the screen, he frowned. Tadeo was one of De Luca's guys. They'd met on the inside and while Kevin hadn't exactly trusted anyone, he and Tadeo had looked out for each other. Kevin had never been officially accepted as part of the other man's crew, but those guys had been all right with him at least. But his friend hadn't been allowed to attend the meeting with De Luca today. The boss had said he wanted to speak to Kevin alone.

He picked up on the second ring. "Hey."

"You're in for the job," Tadeo said.

Kevin didn't bother to hide his surprise with his friend. "You sure? He barely said two words to me."

"I'm sure. If he hadn't liked you, you'd be dead. One of his guards texted me that the job is a go. He's giving you two days to get a plan together then he wants another sit down. A real one. You'll go over the infiltration step by step, leaving nothing to chance. And…you know he'll kill the girl when the job's over."

Kevin frowned. "You never said anything about that."

There was a long moment of silence before Tadeo spoke again. "The inside person always dies. It has to happen this way."

He didn't like it, but didn't push it. "Fine, whatever. The crew will be small and I want you on it for the break-in."

"I'm in," Tadeo said without hesitation.

"Talk to you in a few." Now he had to get serious about pulling this off. And that meant he had to get Ellie's cooperation. This could be his in with De Luca and given time, he planned to take over the man's entire operation. He'd already stolen from him once. The only piece missing now was Ellie.

In the end, he'd get her to cooperate. He always had before. This time he might have to use a little violent persuasion.

CHAPTER FIVE

Ellie felt as if she was going to her execution as she stepped inside their home. Jay had followed her very closely the entire drive back, not that she blamed him. It had taken all her convincing just to let her drive. But in the end, he hadn't wanted her car left at Teaser's so he'd relented.

She'd acted stupid and rash this morning, but she still didn't regret her decision. She didn't want to bring Jay into this mess. It was too dangerous. She didn't care how well trained he was, the man wasn't bulletproof. Unfortunately she knew she didn't have a choice now.

As he stepped inside behind her, he shut the door with more force than necessary before locking it and setting the alarm. When he turned to her, his expression was fierce, his green eyes glittering with anger. "Take off Wyatt's jacket," he growled.

"What?" That was the last thing she'd expected him to say.

"I don't like seeing you in another man's clothing." His words were as raw and real as the pain etched on his face.

Jay had always been a little dominant, something she found she enjoyed, but this was different. It didn't scare her, but this possessive streak was new. She slid the jacket off, hiding a wince of pain as she moved her arms. The action reminded her of her tender ribs.

Of course Jay didn't miss it. His expression immediately softened as he took the jacket and hung it on the pegged rack next to the door. "Let's go to the kitchen."

His concern made her feel even worse for what she'd done. She hated this void she'd created between them and knew there wouldn't be an easy fix. Or a fix at all. She'd made her choice and she expected Jay would want to help her because that's simply the kind of man he was, but now that she'd run out on him he wouldn't want her in his life anymore. Even if he could somehow get past her running, he wouldn't want her after she told him about her past. This was another reason she'd wanted to leave. She couldn't face rejection and worse, disgust, from the only man she'd ever loved.

As she entered the room behind him, he didn't look at her as he said, "Sit."

She sat at the granite cook top island in the middle of the kitchen and leaned back against the swivel chair, trying not to wince. She was sore where that jerk had kicked her. First Jay set a glass of water and two over-the-counter pills for headaches in front of her—but still wouldn't look at her. The back of her skull ached dully from where her hair had been yanked and her ribs throbbed so she gladly took them.

Watching Jay's backside as he opened the freezer, she felt her face flushing as she remembered what they'd done that morning right on this floor, and looked away from him. It wouldn't do to start thinking about the way he'd buried his face between her legs and... She closed her eyes and mentally shook herself. Now that she wanted to think of anything but that, it was all she could envision.

At the sound of him clearing his throat, she opened her eyes to find him hovering above her, almost cautiously. Damp washcloth and ice pack in hand, his jaw was tight. "Can you take off your shirt?" The raspy, unsteady quality of his voice surprised her, but she did as he asked, unbuttoning the only two buttons that hadn't been ripped off.

After taking it off, she crumpled the shirt into a ball and set it on the counter. It would be going in the trash because getting it mended wasn't an option. She never wanted to see it again.

His gaze intense on hers, Jay reached out with one hand and gently pressed against her already bruising ribs. The blackish-purple color was light, but she knew it would get worse with time. "How bad is it?" he asked softly, that stare unnerving.

"Not too bad." Oddly enough, she liked having his hand on her, even in such a tender area.

"I should go back and kill him," he growled before wrapping the ice pack in the thin washcloth.

Reaching out, Ellie grabbed his wrist. "Don't." She was unable to keep the fear out of her voice. If Jay did something and got sent to jail, or worse, because of her… Her throat tightened and those damn tears threatened again.

Jay let out a curse and sat next to her on one of the other swivel chairs. Her throat tightened at the loss of him touching her. Then he surprised her by reaching out and cupping her cheek in one of his big hands. He swiped a callused thumb across her cheek and caught a stray tear she wasn't able to blink back. "I've been taking care of myself for a long damn time. I'm not scared of scum like that." He handed her the wrapped icepack which she gratefully took.

Pressing it against her side, she shivered from the cold. She felt so vulnerable and exposed sitting there in her skimpy bra and skirt.

Jay took a deep breath, as if he was trying to contain the anger she could still see simmering in his green eyes. "It's time to talk. Why'd you run and leave the shittiest note in the world for me to find?"

She swallowed at the now completely unconcealed anger vibrating through his voice. She knew she had no choice but to tell him everything. "This morning I received a call from an ex-boyfriend. We were together when I was seventeen, but he..." Oh, god, this was so embarrassing, but she forged ahead, needing to get it all out at once. "He got sent to prison for felony robbery and thanks to Nevada's three-strike rule he was supposed to have been sent away for a long time. I have no idea how he's out so soon, but he was only in for a little over eight years."

Jay frowned now, his expression darkening. "Have you talked to him since he's been in?"

She shook her head. "Not since I was seventeen. He called collect a few times, but...I wanted to leave him and everything in my past behind when I started college." She left out how she felt she'd deserved to be with someone like Kevin. How it was her fault her sister had gotten killed and how she probably deserved to go to jail for the money she'd used for school.

"So after eight years he calls you after allegedly no contact and you run. Why?" An angry, demanding question.

At the word alleged, her temper spiked, the flare inside her enough that she slammed the icepack on the counter. "It's not alleged! I haven't talked to him in years. I hate him, Jay. But, I...I have something of his. He asked me to hide it for him so I did." Shame filled her, forcing her to look down at her lap. Clasping her hands tightly, she focused on them, watching the way her knuckles turned white. For a moment she wondered why Jay wasn't asking what it was she had, but she quickly realized it was because he wouldn't push her on that point.

Swallowing hard, she met those piercing green eyes even though she didn't want to. "He stole five hundred thousand dollars before he got sent to prison for that robbery." Jay muttered a curse, but she continued. "Kevin was always greedy. He'd just gotten the score of a lifetime and wanted more. It was always more with him." Something she'd only seen in hindsight once she'd been a little older.

"So you still have his money?"

"Most of it." Oh yeah, it was time to come clean, even knowing he'd judge her for the decisions she'd made.

His eyebrows raised at that, but he didn't ask the question she was going to answer anyway. "I'm fifty thousand short. I used about a hundred to pay for school."

He blinked, clearly surprised.

And she felt her defenses rising. "It's how I was able to attend school full time and finish so early. Without having to work I took more than a full load of classes each semester—and had pretty much no life because all I did was study."

"Ellie—"

She cut him off, not wanting to hear his condemnation. "Getting a college degree was important to me! I'm the first in my family to get one." And she was proud of it. Immediately after she'd gotten her bachelor's she'd gone for her master's. "I've replaced half of it already and planned to put the rest back in the next five years. I thought I had more time."

Jay was quiet for a moment, watching her carefully, not exactly assessing, but he was staring as if he was seeing her in a different light. She tightened her jaw and leaned back against the chair, crossing her arms around herself even though it pulled at her sore ribs.

"Who'd he take the money from?" Jay finally asked.

Crap, he was asking all the right questions. "Carlo De Luca."

Jay's eyes widened as he slid off the chair. "Are you kidding me!" He wasn't asking. Turning from her, he placed both hands on the island top and took a deep breath. "Carlo De Luca," he muttered, saying the name like a vile curse. Swiveling, he faced her again. "He threatened to tell De Luca you stole it or you'd been sitting on it or whatever if you didn't do something for him, didn't he?"

She nodded, not surprised he'd come to that conclusion.

"That's why you ran?" he demanded, disbelief in his voice, all over his face.

"Yes!" She jumped off the chair, ignoring the discomfort in her side. "That's exactly why I did. Kevin and De Luca are both dangerous men. Kevin went to jail at freaking twenty because he'd already committed three felonies. And he didn't tell me but I think he murdered the crew that helped him rob De Luca. The man is a monster and I guarantee prison has only made him worse. He wants me to help him steal from the Serafina. I knew if I quit and told him I'd been fired that I'd become useless to him. He'd have no reason to bother me anymore and *you* and everyone I care about wouldn't be a target to him. I'm not sorry for the decision I made!" she shouted, unable to stop the rising pitch of her voice. "You're not a super hero Jay, and he'd come after me hard if I stick around here. That means he'd target *you*, the man I love." Those traitorous tears threatened again but she held them at bay.

Jay stared at her, his breath coming in ragged bursts as he watched her in that unreadable way of his that made her want to squirm. "I don't know if I should kiss you or shake you," he finally muttered. "Why were you at that strip club today?" Something about his tone told her that he already knew the answer. Or had guessed.

"I needed money. I didn't have enough in savings to cover the fifty thousand so I planned to get a quick loan and pay Leonard back after I liquidated some of my retirement funds."

"And you didn't feel comfortable asking me for it? You'd rather run, give up what we have together, than set your stupid fucking pride aside and ask me for the money?" The wounded look on his face sliced her to ribbons.

"I *knew* you'd give it to me. That's not the problem, but I wasn't about to ask you. I just couldn't put you in that kind of danger, Jay. I..." She didn't want to talk about it, but she had no choice. "I couldn't lose someone else. It was my fault Anne Marie died and...I just couldn't lose you too." The words felt like a pathetic attempt to explain so much that she couldn't say to him.

She'd lost her sister, her dad had run out on them after Anne Marie's death, blaming Ellie for everything, and then her mom had died a couple years later from cancer. Her mom had never outright blamed Ellie for her sister's death, but she'd seen the accusing look in her mom's eyes every damn day. The guilt threatened to suffocate her for all the poor decisions she'd made as a teenager and she couldn't let the sins of her past take Jay from her too. Even if she had to live without him, it was better than the alternative. Why couldn't he understand that?

The corners around Jay's eyes tightened and she realized she'd said too much. She'd never told him that her sister's death was her fault. Bracing for the inevitable questions, she was surprised when they didn't come.

"What's this Kevin's last name?"

For a brief moment she thought about not telling him, but knew Jay would find out anyway. "Murrell, but I still don't want you involved in this. I'm going to pay him what I owe him then explain that I was fired from the Serafina. He'll likely be pissed, but he won't have a reason to come after me and he'll have his damn money."

Jay just snorted and reached into his jacket pocket. When he held out his hand, palm up and handed her two familiar diamond earrings, her heart stuttered. "Where...how?"

"Wyatt bought them back," he said, dropping them into her hand.

Ellie ran her free hand over her face. Now she owed him for that too. Her throat tightened and she struggled to find something, anything to say to Jay, but couldn't force the words out.

Finally he broke the silence. "I need to call Wyatt so why don't you go change and get some rest?" He was cold now, remote, and she hated it.

She shook her head. "I don't want—"

"I don't care what you want," he snapped, the tendons in his neck pulled tight as he turned away from her. Though she should have expected it, the verbal shut down was like a slap. Feeling lost and exhausted, she made her way upstairs and tried, but failed, to bury the pain at having ruined everything with Jay. A hot shower wouldn't fix anything, but it might get rid of that strip club stench.

Wyatt nodded once at Iris and Hayden as he entered the security room at the Serafina. Almost immediately they stepped away from the different personnel they were talking to and headed for Iris's office on the east side of the expansive room. Video monitors covered an entire wall and there were eyes on each one. Tuning out the steady hum of activity, he strode down the ramped walkway that looped around to where the offices were, avoiding the trek through the middle of the security area.

He met Iris and Hayden as they reached the door of her office. Smiling at him, despite the tension in the air, Iris brushed her lips over his and it took all his restraint to not take it into something deeper as his instinct demanded. Now was definitely not the time. But he loved that she didn't hide her affection for him. He knew some people thought he'd given her the job because she was his wife, but he didn't care what anyone thought. Former military, trained in too many weapons to count and tough as nails, she was more qualified than anyone he knew.

Once the three of them were inside, he shut the door, then pressed a button on the panel that gave the glass wall overlooking the security pit a frosted look so no one could see inside.

"So Ellie's really okay?" Hayden asked, his concern for his brother's girlfriend real.

"Yeah, she got a little roughed up, but it could have been a hell of a lot worse. I thought Jay was going to kill the owner of Teaser's." He glanced at Iris, who was leaning against the front of her desk, before he looked at Hayden. "I'm going to have Vadim doing a lot of research in the very near future on Leonard Smith, but I need you to make sure Jay won't go after him." Wyatt had seen the look of rage in Jay's eyes and was thankful the man hadn't done more than he had to Smith.

Hayden nodded. "Of course."

"I'm serious. No little visit to rough him up, nothing. He can't be seen near that guy. What I'm about to tell you doesn't leave this room, but Smith's security guy…I know him. I have no idea why he was working at Teaser's, but he's a cop. Or used to be or more likely he's working undercover because he didn't do anything to call in backup or tell Ellie to press charges. I have no idea what the story is and I don't know how Ellie knows him, but he's a witness to me, Ellie, Jay and Brannon being there. We now have a connection to that garbage so make sure Jay stays away."

Expression grim, Hayden nodded. "Got it."

Wyatt semi-relaxed, knowing Hayden would make sure Jay listened to reason. Wyatt planned to tell Jay exactly what he'd told Hayden and Iris, but the man listened to his brother more than anyone. Except Ellie. *Ellie.* He still had no clue what she'd gotten herself into but he was damn sure going to find out. "Where's Vadim?"

Iris's jaw twitched ever so slightly. "He had to take care of something personal, but he did a little digging into Ellie's background. More than what your initial background checks on employees cover. He covered pretty much everything he could find, but what's most interesting is the phone call she received this morning. I'm guessing it was right before she ran. She was on the phone for a little over a minute before the call ended. The owner of the cell phone is Tadeo Bejar—he just got out of prison and runs with Carlo De Luca's crew."

Wyatt let his wife's words sink in. De Luca was a piece of trash Wyatt would love to see run out of his city. There was a criminal element in Vegas Wyatt didn't mind. They broke laws and sometimes caused havoc, but they also took care of the people in their neighborhoods. He could respect that. Things weren't always black and white, something he'd learned at a young age. De Luca was like a cancer who cared for no one but himself. He had a history of violent behavior and his little enterprise had grown steadily over the last five years. Wyatt had been keeping an eye on him and now he planned to do more than that if that bastard had threatened Ellie. "Does she have any ties to De Luca?"

Iris shook her head. "Not that V could find and not that Hayden knows of. Personally, I can't see prim and proper Ellie involved with low life criminals. We'll need to talk to her and Jay though."

As if on cue, Wyatt's phone rang and Jay's number appeared on caller ID. "Hey, I'm with Iris and Hayden, I'm putting you on speaker," he said as he answered, waiting for Jay to okay it.

"Hey, guys." There was an edge to Jay's voice Wyatt had never heard. The man was like titanium under pressure, but not now. "Ellie's upstairs so I'm going to make this quick."

After Jay relayed all the details of why Ellie had run, Wyatt asked, "Does she know if this Kevin is involved with a Tadeo Bejar? He just got out of prison and he's with De Luca's crew."

The silence on the other end seemed to stretch for an eternity. "She didn't mention the name, just that her ex contacted her. Maybe Bejar and Kevin were inside together? Can V—"

"Yeah, I'll have him look into both of them. Go get some rest and take care of Ellie. I'll call you with any updates."

Wyatt knew Jay wanted to argue, but his friend just grunted and hung up. "If Kevin stole from De Luca and is now trying to get in with his crew, there's no way De Luca knows what he did. And there's no way he's going to go to De Luca about Ellie. Even if he lies and says she took his money that means he'd have been sitting on the information for eight years."

"But Kevin still wants her to rob the Serafina," Hayden said.

"It's probably his in with De Luca's crew," Iris continued. "Which is a bold move. He stole this guy's money, but now wants to work with him."

Wyatt nodded, thinking of the clusterfuck that had just been dropped into his lap. He had a ton of paperwork to do and a thousand other things that simply couldn't wait and now one of Vegas's criminal elements wanted to rob him. Using one of his most trusted employees no less. "Send V to see me as soon as he gets back," Wyatt said to Iris, who nodded before tilting her head at Hayden.

The other man quietly left the office, shutting the door behind him. As the door clicked into place Iris wrapped her arms around him and laid her head on his shoulder. "I think you need a hug," she murmured.

He chuckled lightly, some of the tension draining from him at her touch. "I need a big fucking drink. But I'll take the hug anytime."

CHAPTER SIX

Jay pressed his hand against the master bathroom door, curling his fingers against the wood as he listened to the shower running. He'd just gotten off the phone with Wyatt and should be following up with other contacts, doing his own damn research on Ellie's ex, but he didn't want to be anywhere but with her.

The fact that she'd left him raked against his insides like razor wire, but the agony and fear in her voice when she'd told him why she'd left was impossible to ignore. He wanted to be angry with her and he was, sort of, but more than that, he wanted to break through that wall between them. The one that made her think it was okay for her to run away. He loved that she wanted to protect him, but the fear he'd seen in her eyes today was too much. There was nothing she couldn't come to him about, nothing he wouldn't take on to protect her.

He'd also seen self-loathing in her beautiful brown eyes. When she'd confessed that she'd been the reason her sister died, the shame in her expression and body language had been too much. He knew her sister had died in a car accident, but Ellie never talked about her family or her life before college. It was like a giant blank slate.

Every time he tried to push for details she shut down or changed the subject. Didn't matter how hard he tried, Ellie was stubborn. That silence was about to change though. They were going to face this threat head on together.

Stripping off his clothes, he tossed them onto the bed before opening the bathroom door.

"Jay?"

Her petite body was blurred behind the thick glass wall enclosure of the shower.

"Yeah." He sounded gruffer than he'd intended. Clearing his throat he continued, "You okay?"

"Fine." A clipped answer that didn't give him a hint of what she was feeling.

Yeah, she didn't get to hold back anymore. Feeling like a nervous teenager, he strode across the cool tile until he stepped down into the enclosure of their oversized shower. When he'd bought the place he'd had some immediate changes made, including expanding the shower. At almost six and a half feet tall, he liked his damn space.

Ellie's back was to him, her long blonde hair plastered to her back as she stood under the pulsing jet of the shower. But she was completely aware of him. He could see it in the way her back stiffened as he stepped inside. His cock hardened instantly at the sight of her toned, fit body. Compact, curvy and all his. Hell yeah, she was still his. Something he planned to make sure she understood. He didn't care if he had to show her over and over. She was going to understand how important she was to him. What he'd do for her. That they belonged together.

"Did you talk to Wyatt?" she asked. She didn't turn around as he drank in the sight of her smooth back and over the tempting curves of her ass. Water dotted all along her tight body, making him even harder.

"Yeah. He's aware of the situation." But he didn't want to discuss the details of that conversation now. "Why did you say your sister's death was your fault?" he asked as he settled his hands on her slender hips.

Her entire body pulled taut and she tried to shift away from him, but he held firm. She wasn't getting away from him this time. Pulling her back to him, he savored the little gasp of surprise she made at the feel of his cock against her back. Leaning down, he nipped at her ear as water rushed over him. "Why are you surprised by my reaction?"

Even above the sound of the water he could hear her swallow hard. "I'm not. It's just biology," she said in a rush.

Bullshit it was. "So you think the sight of any naked woman would make me hard?" He teased her earlobe with his teeth, knowing his calmness would get her riled up.

"They better not," she snapped, then seemed to remember herself. "Jay, what are you doing?"

He rolled his hips against her. "You really need me to explain?" he asked as he slipped one hand from her hip over her flat belly, then lower, lower until he cupped her mound.

"This...don't you...aren't you angry at me?" Her voice shook, getting worse when he gently rubbed his middle finger over her clit.

"I'm *furious*, baby. But that doesn't change what's between us." And he planned to strengthen their bond in every possible way he could.

"But..." She sucked in a breath when he increased the pressure of his finger ever so slightly. "Don't you want me gone? Or is this about a last...time? Angry sex?" She whispered the last couple words, her voice wobbling.

Which only pissed him off more. He stopped stroking but held her tight. "You think I'd do that?" He couldn't keep the anger from his voice now even if he'd wanted to.

"No! I just don't understand why you still want me after the way I ran. Especially now that you know all about my past. I used stolen money to pay for school, my ex was a criminal and I...I did so many stupid things that you shouldn't want me." Her head dropped, almost as if she was ashamed again.

Everyone did stupid things, especially when they were young. He would never judge her for her past—he was in love with who she was now and he wanted the whole package. Not some sanitized version of herself she seemed to think he needed. "What happened with your sister?"

She was silent so long he figured he'd pushed too hard too fast, had miscalculated by asking now. When she spoke though, her voice was harsh and bitter. "In high school I was a bit of a geek. Not un-liked or un-popular, but back then I was shy and hadn't quite grown into myself and much preferred studying to going out on weekends. When I was sixteen a couple girls from my study group convinced me to go to a party one Saturday. It was fun enough and I had a good time, but I drank more than I realized. I was even smaller then so you can imagine my tolerance."

She shrugged, her laugh sounding hollow and packed full of years of anger. "I was terrified of how my dad would react—which considering he was an alcoholic, I can now appreciate the irony—so I called my sister. She was four years older than me and had moved out right at eighteen. Anne Marie was so beautiful. Tall, willowy, looked just like our mom. And she could *dance.* Could have gone to any professional school in the world, but she loved Vegas. Absolutely loved it here."

The pain intermixed with love in her voice was so real it punched right through Jay. He'd never heard Ellie talk so openly about her family. "At twenty she was already headlining one of the biggest shows on the strip. She had her whole life ahead of her..." Ellie trailed off and Jay tightened his hold, wrapping his arms around her waist. She melted against him, trembling.

"You don't have to continue." He buried his face against the back of her head, inhaling the subtle vanilla scent of her recently shampooed hair.

She took a shuddering breath. "Yes, I do. I'm sure you can fill in the rest anyway. She died in an accident on the way to pick me up. It wasn't a drunk driver either. Just an accident. There was no one to blame but me. If I hadn't been drinking and stuck for a ride, she wouldn't have died."

"It wasn't your fault." He knew his words would fall on deaf ears, but he had to say them anyway. He couldn't believe she'd lived with that kind of guilt for so long.

She snorted. "Yeah well, my father certainly thought so. He split a week after her funeral and made sure I knew it was because of what I'd done. *I* ripped the family apart, he said. *I* was killing our mother. *I'd* killed Anne Marie. *I* should have been the one who died," she whispered the last part.

"Damn it." Jay turned Ellie around, pulling her out of the spray of water and stepping under it so he'd block her from the steady onslaught. "Look at me."

She did, but her hands were still at her sides, as if she was afraid to touch him. The fear he saw in her gaze was too much. Fear that he'd reject her. It made his chest ache. "You were sixteen doing things stupid sixteen-year-olds do. And it wasn't even that stupid. You drank too much—probably for the first time ever—and were smart enough to call someone to get you. Her death was tragic, but you're not to blame. And your father putting all that on *you*? Fuck him. He left his family after a terrible tragedy. That makes him a gutless bastard." Jay couldn't fathom blaming a kid, his own kid at that, after something so tragic.

Ellie placed tentative hands on his chest, but it wasn't the possessive hold he craved. It was almost as if she wanted to push him away. Instead she slightly dug her fingers into his flesh and relief slid through him that she chose to tighten her grip. "You're saying things I know on an intellectual level but it doesn't change the fact that my sister's dead and it was my fault. Not long after her death I started dating Kevin and..." Closing her eyes, she laid her cheek against his chest.

He definitely didn't need to hear the rest of that. Not yet. He figured she'd likely been eaten up by guilt and had taken the scraps of some asshole who she felt like she deserved. That alone killed him, but he understood. His own younger brother had gone through a dark phase when he'd been forced to retire from the Teams because of an injury.

Jay wrapped his arms around Ellie's body and ran a hand down her back, not stopping until he gripped her ass in a tight, possessive hold. The action took her by surprise and her head jerked back. Even as he was careful not to jostle her because of her ribs, he didn't loosen his grip.

Slowly, giving her plenty of time to stop him, he leaned down. Her dark eyes widened, but it was impossible to miss the unmistakable flare of need in her gaze. Even if it was intermixed with surprise.

He never wanted to see that expression on her face in reaction to him wanting her. She might be preparing for the worst no matter what he said, for him to leave or kick her out after this, but it wasn't happening.

Stroking his tongue against hers, he shuddered as she melted into him, into the kiss, completely giving herself to him. Ellie was always like that. All he had to do was kiss or touch her right and she molded around him like he was the only thing that mattered. As if she couldn't get enough of him.

Which was good because the feeling was mutual. Ellie had gotten under his skin from the moment he'd met her. Jay had already been working for Wyatt a few years when his boss had hired Ellie. Fresh out of college, the brown-eyed little vixen had nearly bowled him over. He'd had so many damn fantasies about her it was embarrassing.

She was an absolute work-a-holic leaving little time for play, but he'd bided his time. With all the out of town trips they went on together with their boss, he'd ended up spending more time with her than anyone else in his life. They'd become good friends, but he'd wanted more. He'd known she had too, but still, she'd kept the friendship boundaries strictly in place until over a year ago in Miami when he'd almost died in an explosion.

Since then he'd been inside her every chance he got. Each time he was with her his need grew. The woman was a complete addiction he never wanted to get over. Right now he knew he couldn't be gentle if she let him inside her tight body, but that didn't mean he couldn't please her.

As he kissed his way along her jaw, she arched into him, brushing her already hard nipples against his chest.

"Jay," she murmured as he reached that sensitive area along her collarbone. He raked his teeth against her skin and she wrapped her fingers around his cock, squeezing with just enough pressure to drive him insane. She stroked once, twice, then he pulled back, his breathing ragged.

Staring up at him, the briefest hint of hurt bled into her eyes. He shook his head, and blindly reaching behind him, he turned down the pressure on the shower so that it was on the lowest setting.

"Sit on the edge," he rasped out, nodding at the built-in bench.

She paused for only a second before doing as he said.

"Now spread your legs," he said as he knelt in front of her.

Her espresso-colored eyes grew heavy-lidded as she complied. She clearly had no doubt what he was about to do and welcomed it. Despite everything that had happened today, the one thing between them that had never been in question was chemistry. Something he wanted to remind her of.

Without touching her, he drank in the sight of her bare body, covered in rivulets of water, faint steam from the leftover heat rising around her. Pale ropes of her hair fell around her full breasts, her pink nipples beading even tighter under his sweeping gaze.

His cock was a heavy club between his legs, but he forced his mind off his own need as he ran his palms along the inside of her legs, moving from her knees up to her inner thighs. Gently, slowly, he ran his thumbs along her soft lips.

She shuddered, placing her hands on his shoulders as if she would stop him. But she just clutched on to him, her fingernails digging into his skin as she urged him on.

Leaning down, he inhaled her sweet scent as he opened her pink folds.

"Don't tease, Jay," she whispered, her voice unsteady, her body practically shaking as his lips brushed against her sensitive skin.

Showing her complete lack of patience, another thing he loved about her, she scooted farther past the edge of the bench, practically shoving herself at his mouth.

Smiling against her slickness, he stroked his tongue along her slit and was rewarded with a pure moan of pleasure from Ellie. He knew he should tease her, draw this out as long as possible, but he needed to make her come.

Needed to feel her pleasure coating his tongue. Needed to hear his damn name on her lips and know she craved him as much as he did her.

He dipped his tongue inside her, stroking and teasing. With his thumb, he began rubbing her clit in tight little circles, knowing it would push her to the edge even faster.

Her breathing grew even more ragged as her hands moved from his shoulders to his head. She slid her fingers along his buzz cut, holding his head as she moaned. "Oh...right...there." Her words were broken and uneven.

He wanted more.

With his other hand he slid two fingers inside her, pushing fast and deep. She nearly vaulted off the slick tile of the bench before lifting one leg and throwing it over his back. With her spread out like that, he was in an even better position to give her exactly what she needed.

Moving his fingers in and out of her, he played her body with precision until she was coming against his mouth and saying his name like a prayer in the most ragged voice. As her slickness coated his fingers, her inner walls convulsing as her climax punched through her, he practically growled in triumph against her slit.

He hadn't realized how much he'd needed this from her until he tasted her desire. Her fingers, which had been digging into his skull, loosened and she stroked her hands over his head and down to his shoulders. "Thank you, Jay," she whispered.

He didn't want her thanks, he wanted her trust, her heart. Instead of responding, he kissed his way up her flat stomach, careful of her side, and not stopping until he reached her mouth. He claimed her lips, teasing his tongue against hers with barely concealed restraint. More than anything he wanted to slide his cock into her, to take her roughly against the tile, but with her ribs, he wouldn't.

She must have sensed it because she slid off the bench so that she was kneeling in front of him. Reaching between their bodies, she fisted his hard length and started stroking him.

He felt like he should tell her to stop...for some reason. His brain short circuited as he tried to think of a reason why. There was none. He continued kissing her, branding her the only way he could as she caressed him.

Just the taste of her on his tongue was enough to set him off, but feeling her hands on his body was too much. He tore his mouth from hers, staring into her eyes as she continued stroking him. He wanted her to see him at his most vulnerable, to show her what she meant to him, how much he trusted her. Her dark eyes were heavy-lidded as she watched him, pumped him, and brought him to a toe-numbing orgasm. The feel of her elegant fingers stroking his cock made him want to hold off longer because he didn't want to give up her touch. As the climax built, becoming too much, he buried his face against her neck as he came, shuddering and groaning under the onslaught of his orgasm.

He'd never felt such an intense connection to anyone until Ellie. Everything about her called to him on the most primal level.

After he caught his breath, he pulled back to find her watching him carefully. She smiled tentatively, almost nervously, and he could tell she wanted to ask him something. "What is it, baby?"

She bit her bottom lip, the action so un-Ellie like it floored him. "What *are* we now? What's going to happen between us?"

"You mean are we still together?"

She nodded.

His first instinct was to be annoyed at the question, but he knew it was coming from a place of vulnerability. "Yes...but I don't know what's going to happen." He knew exactly what *he* wanted from Ellie, but until she trusted him, until she decided that they'd face any and all problems together as a team, he didn't know what the future held because that was up to her to decide.

Hurt flickered in her gaze before she stood quickly and turned away from him. Hand on the shower knob, she said, "I'm going to turn up the pressure so we can wash off."

He stood too, moving out of the way so the stream didn't slam into his face. They washed off together in silence, and he hated how he could see her practically building a wall between them again. Slapping the mortar on and laying the bricks one at a time.

"I didn't say I didn't love you, Ellie." His words seemed harsh, over-pronounced in the enclosure.

Her dark gaze snapped up to meet his, but she didn't respond. Just stared at him questioningly.

"I don't know what's going to happen between us because that's up to *you*. When you figure it out, let me know." He wasn't going to spell it out for her. He knew what he wanted; it was time for her to decide if she wanted the same thing. Because he had some damn pride. Without waiting for a response, he left the shower, snagging a towel from the nearest hook as he went.

CHAPTER SEVEN

Ellie wrapped the dark green silky robe Jay had bought for her a couple months ago around her body and stumbled toward the bedroom. Her damp hair hung down her back, soaking through the material and giving her a chill, but she didn't care enough to dry it. She felt raw and ripped open and it was her own damn fault. She could read through the lines, and understood what Jay hadn't said in the shower.

God, she was so screwed up. She didn't understand why Jay even wanted her. Especially after everything she'd told him. But he'd basically said the ball was in her court. And she'd hurt him yet again, without even meaning to.

Sighing and pushing thoughts of her own dysfunction aside, she grabbed her cell from her purse and sat on the bed. Even though she didn't want to, she turned it back on. As expected it started pinging out of control, indicating multiple texts and voicemails. She listened to her messages first and was surprised that they were all work-related. Maybe Wyatt had been serious about not letting her go because all the calls were from people who should have known she'd quit by now. Of course there was one from Sierra and Iris, both sounding concerned about her. Which meant they likely knew everything.

She groaned at the thought. Sierra was so sweet and freaking innocent she probably thought Ellie was a drama queen or...Ellie didn't know what, but it couldn't be good. And Iris was Wyatt's wife. Beautiful, wealthy, so put together. The woman had probably never seen a trailer park or had any contact with the types of people Ellie had run with so long ago. She could only imagine what Iris thought and it made her cringe. She'd worked so hard to build a new life for herself, leave all the shady stuff behind.

Ellie ran her palm over her face. She desperately needed to fix things with Jay. The problem was, she didn't know where to start. She felt almost like a stranger around him. And it was all her fault. She also needed to get her act together and call Wyatt, but...she still wasn't sure what the right decision was. If she worked at the Serafina, she put everyone in danger. There had to be a way out of this. Of course, first she needed to give Kevin his money. Jay had said he'd help her out so maybe once she gave the money to Kevin and said she didn't work at the Serafina any longer things could work out.

Laying back against the pillows, she scrolled through her texts, responding to the work-related ones that she could. Once she'd done that, she opened the texts from the same number Kevin had called her from. At first they were almost innocuous. *Call me. We need to talk.* Then they escalated into threatening. *Call me bitch. I want what's mine or else.*

Yeah, that sounded like the winner she knew. Closing her eyes, she set the phone on the fluffy comforter next to her and massaged her temple. There had to be a way out of this mess. A way that no one she loved got hurt.

To figure that out, she needed to talk to Jay. Because he was right to put this on her. She needed to work with him to figure out this mess then go from there. He deserved someone who trusted him enough not to run the way she had. She might not ever work through her issues or truly deserve a man like Jay but she had to try. He was the best thing that had ever happened to her and she didn't want to go through life without him.

She would talk to him…in just a couple minutes. Exhaustion swept over her as the comfortable bed molded to her body. She was safe, in the home she shared with the man she loved and all she wanted to do was sleep. Just for ten minutes. Then she'd deal with the big mess she'd gotten herself into.

Ellie popped up from the waiting room chair as the doctor strode in, his expression the same flat one it always seemed to be. She'd been suffocating in here as they waited for news on Jay. After that terrible explosion at Wyatt's Miami mansion Jay had been knocked unconscious. Or maybe he was in a coma. They simply didn't know what was going on and the stupid doctors weren't giving them updates fast enough.

Dr. Warren cleared his throat. "Mr. Wentworth is going to be okay. He has a concussion, a few stitches on his head and some broken ribs but he's going to pull through. He's awake now and asking to see Ellie. Normally I wouldn't allow visitors—"

Ellie elbowed Wyatt out of the way as she hurried to stand directly in front of the doctor. She couldn't believe Jay was asking to see her, especially since they weren't a couple, but she was desperate to see him. "I'm Ellie."

Dr. Warren fingered his stethoscope for a moment, then sighed. "He's not very coherent and—"

"I don't care. If he's awake enough to ask for me I want to see him." She didn't care how desperate she sounded or that anyone knew about her feelings for Jay.

The doctor sighed again and motioned that she should follow him. She barely remembered the walk to his room, could only focus on the clicking sound of her heels until finally the older man stopped in front of a partially open door and indicated she could enter.

Steeling herself for the sight of Jay injured, she pushed open the door. The room was dimly lit as she stepped inside. Her heart jumped into her throat as she moved past the bathroom door and saw him lying on the stark white sheets of the hospital bed.

"Hey," he rasped out, those devilish green eyes of his looking electric against his paler than normal skin.

"Jay. How are you feeling?" Rushing to his side, she hovered at the edge of the bed next to him. He was so big he took up practically the whole thing, his long legs looking cramped at the end. She didn't want to sit and accidentally hurt him.

"Better now that you're here." Before she could move to grab a chair, he snagged her around the waist and pulled her down next to him.

He groaned in discomfort as he half-turned on his side so she had room. "What are you doing?" She didn't move because she didn't want to jostle him further.

"Need you close," he murmured, patting her knee.

"Oh, Jay." She reached out and gently traced the area on his forehead above the long line of stitches. "You are so lucky." Her throat tightened as she thought about how fortunate he truly was. Broken ribs, stitches and a concussion sucked, but he would heal. The ribs would be the worst, but she planned to be there for him while he got back on his feet.

"I'm fine," he muttered, his words thick and a little slurred. "I could leave tonight."

Unable to stop herself, she snorted. "All right superman, I guess you'll just have to humor the doctors and me and stay put for a few more days, okay?"

"If it makes you happy I'll stay here." He gave her a lopsided smile that made him look so boyish.

She wondered what drugs they had him on, if any. He was hooked up to an IV, but that could just be fluids. "It makes me very happy to know you're being so well taken care of. I was so worried about you." That being an understatement. She'd been ready to take off her boss's head in an attempt to get to Jay after the explosion.

"Worried enough that you'll finally go on that first date with me?" His gaze narrowed, some of the sleepiness falling away.

"Yes."

He blinked in surprise. "Yes? Just like that?"

She nodded, her throat tightening again. God, she could have lost him before they'd ever had a chance to start. She'd been attracted to him from the moment she'd met him, but they worked together so that had made him off limits. Lately he'd been pushing harder and her resolve had been weakening to the point she'd almost kissed him earlier today. "Just like that."

"I would've blown myself up a long time ago if I'd known that's all it would take to get you to go out with me."

Laughing, she reached out and stroked the side of his face, cupping his cheek gently. "Don't even joke about that."

He covered her hand with his big one, that boyish grin playing across his face making him seem a decade younger as he leaned his face into her hold.

He opened his mouth to speak and an explosion rumbled beneath them...

Ellie's eyes flew open and she jerked upright in bed. Breathing hard, she looked around her and Jay's bedroom feeling lost and disoriented. What the hell? She'd been dreaming about Jay... How long had she been out? Glancing at her cell phone she realized it hadn't been very long. Her hair was still damp too.

She rubbed a hand over her face and slid her legs off the bed. She needed to get up and—the bedroom door flew open and she nearly jumped out of her skin.

Jay stood there in jeans, no shirt and a gun held tightly in his hand. Her eyes widened, not because of the gun, but because he was clearly agitated. "Pack a bag. Someone just blew up your car."

"What?" No way she'd heard him correctly.

Mouth pulled into a grim line, he nodded. "Pack enough for a couple weeks. I've called the cops and Wyatt, but you and I are getting the hell out of here and somewhere safer until this mess is sorted out."

Feeling numb, she moved toward the closet. Her car had been parked in the driveway. Someone had come to their home and done this. She or Jay could have been badly injured, or worse. "Was anyone hurt? Did you see who did it?"

He shook his head. "No to both counts."

At least no one had been injured, but if someone had blown up her car—and she had no doubt who had done it—things had just gotten a lot more deadly. "It had to be Kevin, right?"

Jay nodded. "That's my guess."

She paused by the closet door and clutched onto it, thankful for the support. She knew she needed to pack and that they had to get the hell out of there, but she felt almost frozen, her limbs numb. "What are we going to do?"

"Get some place safe, regroup with a team, and take this bastard down." The razor's edge to his voice sent a chill down her spine.

Ellie had seen Jay intense at work before, especially with the various threatening situations they dealt with, but she'd never seen him like this. So...deadly.

It completely melted her that he'd do anything to protect her, but her nightmare was coming to life. Jay was now involved and in real danger.

Because of her.

CHAPTER EIGHT

Kevin grinned at the sight of Ellie's car engulfed in flames. As Tadeo turned the corner, leaving her street, he faced forward. Some neighbors had come out of their homes and he didn't want to be seen paying too much attention to the car.

"That'll get her to call me back." She'd been ignoring his calls and texts all day. He hadn't cared much before his meeting with De Luca because he'd thought he'd had time. Not two days to get a plan together to rob the Serafina. Not the actual casino of course. Anyone stupid enough to try to rob a casino vault deserved to get a bullet to the head.

"You better hope so, *mano*." Tadeo shook his head.

Kevin didn't understand why Tadeo called him and practically everyone *mano*, slang for brother. He wasn't his fucking family.

Tadeo continued, sounding slightly stressed. "I'd have never told De Luca you had a plan before you locked your girl down. Why didn't you tell me she wasn't solid?"

"She's not my girl." The words were automatic. And if they planned on killing her after the job—he hadn't decided if he was going to let that happen yet or not—he wanted to keep his distance from her.

"You know what I mean." Tadeo rolled his eyes as he took another turn down a quiet dead end street still in the same nice neighborhood and parked.

They were driving one of De Luca's cars, a light gray minivan that looked like something a soccer mom would drive. Which was exactly the point. They had to blend in. And this place was higher-middle class. Definitely on the high end. And she'd gotten here because she'd used his money. For school probably, knowing her. She'd always been so brainy, which was actually hot. "It's not a big deal. I'll lock her in with the plan. She just needs some persuasion. Besides, all we need is a clean exit after we grab those jewels. She's Christiansen's personal assistant. She can make it happen."

"Maybe." Tadeo didn't sound sure, which annoyed Kevin, but he let it roll off his back.

For now. He was in control of this heist and it was just the beginning before he created his empire. It would take time, but he was patient. He hadn't gotten out of prison early by dumb luck. Tadeo didn't know it, but Kevin had flipped on a couple guys on the inside. That's what people got for bragging about their crimes. They deserved everything that came their way for their pure stupidity.

"Not maybe. Now that we've scared her she'll contact me. All she's gotta do is give me a little information and we're golden. I know how to convince her so don't worry about it." She'd created a cushy little life for herself and she wouldn't want her friends and boyfriend to know how she'd gotten there. He'd just make her see things his way.

"I have to worry. If this deal falls through it looks bad on me too. De Luca doesn't forgive easy." There was raw fear in Tadeo's voice that Kevin had never heard before.

Even though Kevin was afraid of that bastard too, he shrugged. He wasn't going to show his fear. That's what made him different than Tadeo. Besides, he had a backup plan. He'd just run with the money he'd taken years ago if it came down to it. Hell, he couldn't believe Ellie still had most of it. He wouldn't have saved it for anyone. Which told him that she must still care about him a little. Maybe he could use that to his advantage too.

Threaten her, scare her, break her down, then build her up again. He'd seen that in prison too many times to count. First he needed to find out more about this boyfriend though. He couldn't see Ellie settling down with some pussy, but maybe this suit was all part of her new lifestyle. The guy was big yeah, but that didn't mean shit.

Multiple cop cars and a fire truck flew by, heading toward Ellie's place, their sirens blaring. "I need more information on Christiansen's main guard." The file De

Luca had on the man was pathetic. In fact, the files he had on Christiansen were slim too. Apparently De Luca hated the man enough to have files on him, which Kevin found interesting. But it wouldn't do him any good without more details.

Tadeo snorted. "You mean your girl's live-in *boyfriend*? Man, I'll see what I can do, but De Luca has tried to get as much as he can on all Christiansen's inner circle and it's damn near impossible. They've all got top secret files or some shit."

"Top secret? Like with the government?"

He just shrugged. "Man, how would I know? De Luca doesn't tell me that shit."

"Why does De Luca have a hard-on for Christiansen anyway?" He had to, otherwise he wouldn't want to target the man's casino.

"The rich guy bought up a bunch of property he wanted and Christiansen's made it known what he thinks of De Luca. I think it's a pride thing. Pride and money. Those jewels are worth like, millions."

Kevin resisted snorting. Sometimes he forgot how uneducated Tadeo was. In prison Kevin had taken advantage of the system and gotten his bachelor's and he read everything he could get his hands on. "They're priceless." Which meant De Luca could net anything on the black market if he put them up for auction. Christiansen had them on loan from a German museum as part of a bigger display showcasing and celebrating art from all over the world. And those jewels were considered art, they were so beautiful. Even Kevin could appreciate them.

"Whatever, *mano*. They're worth a lot of money." When another cop car cruised past, Tadeo started the engine and pulled out onto the main street that would lead them out of the neighborhood.

Kevin frowned. "What are you doing?" They were supposed to stay and wait to follow Ellie and her boyfriend after she left.

"There're too many cops. I don't like the way this feels so I'm not staying."

For a moment Kevin started to argue, but then he nodded. "Yeah, all right." He wouldn't question Tadeo's gut. After going to prison, he knew better. That was all right, he wasn't letting Ellie get away from him that easily.

***

Ellie wrapped her arms around herself, shivering in the passenger seat as Jay drove them to the Serafina. But it wasn't from the cold. Someone, she was ninety-nine percent sure it was Kevin, had blown up her car. But to what end? To scare her into cooperating? It did scare her, but more than anything it pissed her off.

Taking her by surprise because of his almost distant attitude when they'd been at the police station, Jay reached out and squeezed her knee once, never taking his gaze from the road. "We're going to be very safe soon."

"I know, I just don't like that you've been dragged into this mess." When he frowned, she hurried on. "Not because I think you can't handle yourself." She realized, belatedly, that earlier she'd likely insulted him in a way she hadn't thought of. She knew he was capable. The man was trained and deadly, but she was still terrified of him getting caught in the crossfire. "And I don't like that we lied to the police." Jay had instructed her not to mention Kevin's calls.

"We didn't lie. You just omitted some information."

She sighed, staring out the window at the bright lights as they cruised down the main strip. They were only minutes from the Serafina. "I know and I know why we did, it just felt weird." If she told them about Kevin, they might eventually learn about that money. Of course, De Luca had never reported it stolen because he'd likely laundered or stolen it himself. But Jay didn't want her tied to Kevin at all.

"Trust me, this will work out." He sounded so confident and sure that it would.

She just wished she could believe it. When her phone buzzed in her purse, she pulled it out. Her stomach dropped the moment she saw the message. "He just texted me again."

Jay shot her a sharp look as he turned down the quiet side street that would lead to one of the private employee parking garages at the back of the casino. "What did he say?"

"He asked if I was ready to talk now."

"Now that he's blown up your car?" Jay muttered as he slowed at the private gate and punched in his employee code.

"I should call him back now." She needed to hear exactly what he wanted from her. Maybe she could convince Kevin that the money would be enough.

"Just wait ten more minutes." Jay had been cryptic about his plan and she hadn't wanted to push him. He was already on edge and she had to trust him. He was definitely more trained for negotiations than her. And she assumed that's what he wanted to do.

After they parked, they used one of the private elevators and stopped when they reached the sixtieth floor. She'd been up here when she was given a tour of the place and once after when escorting a big client for Wyatt. Occasionally Wyatt opened it up to the Serafina's high rollers, but the ten floors above this one were where the whales usually stayed. No, this one was for non-gambling and non-casino related clients. Wyatt's businesses were so diverse and he kept this floor for his personal use.

"Is this where we're staying?" she asked as they exited into a tiled area with real gold trim around each piece of tile.

"Yeah." He nodded at the hallway where a long carpet runner reached from one set of elevators to the others on the opposite side.

Falling in step with Jay, she tried to calm the nerves dancing in her belly, but it was no use. She wanted to know what Jay's plan was and more than anything, she wanted this nightmare behind her and all the people she cared about safe.

As they reached the halfway point in the hallway, Jay slowed and the door opened to reveal Hayden. He must have been watching for them. Or maybe Jay had texted him that they'd arrived.

Hayden took one of the rolling suitcases and Jay wrapped an arm around her shoulders. "Is everyone here?" he asked, pulling her tight against him.

She was thankful for the small show of support. She didn't know what to expect right then and was glad that despite his annoyance and anger with her, Jay was showing her that she could count on him.

"Yeah." Hayden nodded and gave Ellie a half-smile before stepping back so they could come in.

Jay left the other bag near the front door as Hayden shut it and locked it behind them. Ellie could hear the low hum of voices as they strode down the short interior hallway to the living room. The room was decorated with a simplistic style, but there were splashes of vibrant color in all the accent pieces. She wasn't surprised to see the long drapes covering the 12 foot windows pulled closed. She was surprised, however, to see Iris and Vadim there waiting with Wyatt. Jay hadn't said much on the drive over, and she wondered if he knew they'd be here.

Unfortunately one quick glance at his hard expression didn't reveal anything. Since the explosion he'd been in what she called battle mode. The man didn't reveal anything.

"Hey hon, how're you feeling?" Iris asked, the woman's uncharacteristically soft voice and expression taking Ellie off guard.

Throat tight, she nodded, touched by Iris's concern. "Good...okay, that's a lie. I'm terrified." That being an understatement.

Jay squeezed her shoulders again and she leaned into him. The man was an absolute rock. Her rock, if she'd let him be. Iris murmured understanding as Jay nodded at the living room. "Let's sit."

Ellie made her way to the plush, bright pink chaise that should have been a ridiculous color but somehow fit with the rest of the room. A sparkly chandelier hung high in the middle of the room, its soft glow illuminating everything while creating a peaceful atmosphere. As Jay sat next to her, she cuddled up next to him.

He jerked a little as if surprised, but immediately pulled her into the safety of his arms, wrapping both of them around her. "It's going to be okay," he murmured quietly against the top of her head, for her ears only.

Wyatt—who Ellie had been avoiding eye contact with since she'd entered—sat next to Iris on a longer couch, and Vadim and Hayden sat on two single chairs angled toward the glass coffee table.

"We're going to take care of this," Wyatt said, his voice steady and determined.

Ellie met his gaze to find no censure there. The relief that slid through her was potent. "I'm sorry I—"

Wyatt just shook his head. "I understand why you ran. You wanted to protect those you care about and I can respect that. Just don't do it again. I'm already losing my mind without you and…" He trailed off as Iris nudged him. "Anyway, do you know a Tadeo Bejar?"

She shook her head. With how many people she dealt with daily, she was very good at names and faces and that name wasn't familiar. "No, should I?"

"He's the owner of the phone your ex called you from. They both did time together, and got out of prison around the same time. So, they're in on whatever scheme they're running together."

"Okay."

"Bejar is part of Carlo De Luca's crew." Wyatt watched her carefully as he spoke, as if looking for a reaction.

All she felt was pure shock. "What? Kevin robbed—" She shot a quick glance at Jay who just nodded that yes, he'd told Wyatt everything. He hadn't told her all the details he'd covered with their boss and she wanted to make sure. She looked back at everyone, feeling uncomfortable being in the spotlight. "That doesn't make sense. Kevin robbed De Luca before he went to prison, but as far as I know De Luca doesn't know." It had been years ago, back before De Luca had the crew he did now. He'd still been dangerous, but his reputation was even worse now. And she knew it was one based on truth.

Wyatt was silent for a long moment. "And he wants his money back." Not a question.

"Yeah. And before you ask, it's somewhere safe." Even Jay hadn't asked her where it was and she didn't plan on sharing that information even with him. Not because she didn't trust him, or any of them, but because if she told them the location, they'd become even more involved than they needed to be.

"Why'd you keep it all these years? Especially if he wasn't supposed to be out for another couple decades." Iris asked.

"Fear." Ellie's answer was instant. "I could be fifty when he'd gotten out and if that money wasn't waiting for him, he'd kill me."

Wyatt glanced at Vadim. He gave the pale-eyed man a subtle nod. Apparently that was the computer genius's cue because he half-smiled at Ellie, though it was more of a baring of teeth. V was nice enough, but if she was being truly honest, the Russian scared her in a way she couldn't define. She wasn't afraid he'd hurt her and she'd seen how sweet he was with one of the waitresses who worked at Sierra's restaurant, but something about him screamed that he was a predator—and everyone else was prey. It was unnerving to say the least.

"We want you to call Kevin back," he said, just the barest hint of an accent in his voice. "I'm going to record and attempt to track the call."

She had no clue how that was possible but she was pretty sure it was illegal. Ellie looked at Jay, who nodded and said, "This is all part of our plan. We want to find out what Kevin's end game is and we want you to agree to help him. If V can lock onto his signal now, he'll be able to keep better tabs on him from this point forward."

Her eyes widened. "You want me to agree to help him rob the casino?"

"Depending on what he asks, yes. But you can't seem too eager or agree right away or he'll get suspicious."

"Okay, then what?"

"Then we'll make a decision from there," Wyatt said.

Even though the thought of talking to Kevin made her skin crawl, she nodded. "I'll call him whenever you want." She pulled her cell phone from her jacket pocket and held it out to Vadim. "How are you going to record the call?"

With a practically gleeful smile, he took it. "Just give me a moment."

It wasn't exactly an answer. She watched as he retrieved a small black bag, removed a slim black device that looked like a magnet and some other small black boxes that she had no clue what they were. He laid everything on the glass table, snapped the magnet looking thing to the back of her phone then handed it to her. Moving quickly, he typed in commands on his ultra-thin computer and plugged in the boxes together and joined them to his laptop with a cord. Yeah, this definitely wasn't legal. Finally he nodded at her.

She wiped a damp palm on her jeans before looking at Jay for support. She hated that everyone would have to hear this conversation, or at least her half of it right now, especially Jay. But there was no choice.

"You can do this, baby." That deep, encouraging voice of his rolled over her.

Taking a deep breath, she called the number Kevin had called her from.

He picked up on the first ring. "Took you long enough. You hang up on me again and you'll lose more than just your car."

Just hearing his voice made fear detonate inside her. "What do you want?" she asked, sounding much braver than she actually felt, especially since he'd basically just admitted to bombing her car. The only reason she had any courage right now was because of Jay's presence. She hated that he was hearing all this, but she was grateful he was so close.

"My money and your help taking The Dragon Collection." He was all arrogance, just like she remembered.

It took a moment for his words to register. Then she started laughing, as if he was stupid. Because he was. "You're insane!"

The Dragon Collection was a set of eight rare green diamonds, all a little over seven carats each. When they'd first been discovered, the man who'd found them had said they looked like dragon eyes. The name had stuck. Currently the stunning display was in a very secure room at the casino as part of an international celebration of artwork. The display was open to the public for a small viewing fee and Ellie knew they'd earned a nice bit of revenue from the showing. Individually each diamond was valued at twenty million dollars. Together, they were pretty much priceless. And Kevin thought he was smart enough to steal them. That alone was enough to make her dissolve into hysterical laughter.

But Wyatt nodded that she should agree. Steeling herself, she hoped Kevin bought what she was about to dish out.

Before he could respond, she continued. "I'll give you your money but I'm not helping you with some stupid scheme."

"If you don't help me, the next time a car explodes, your boyfriend will be in it. Money or no money, you'll do what I want."

Her blood chilled at Kevin's angry threat. She couldn't even think about something happening to Jay. "Don't threaten me," she snapped. "Or him." In a fair fight, Jay could take Kevin without breaking a sweat. But she knew all too well that Kevin never fought fair.

"You've built a cushy little life for yourself and if you want to keep it, you're going to help me. If you don't, people you care for will…" He trailed off, letting her fill in the rest. "Come on, Ellie. I don't even need you for much. I just need the layout of the building and the guards' schedule. I know there are multiple shift changes during the day and all I need is the evening schedule."

"That's all you need?" She knew her question would sound like she was bending.

"For now. After a meeting I have Monday I'll need more, but that's it right now. It's easy, Ellie baby."

"Don't call me that," she snapped, the endearment making her skin crawl.

He snorted. "Whatever. You gonna get me what I want or do you want to let innocent people get hurt?"

She paused, as if she was thinking it over. Finally she let out a long sigh. "Fine. I'll see what I can do, but no promises. And I'm holding on to your money. I don't trust you not to kill me."

He started to respond, but she cut him off. "Save it," she muttered. "Can I reach you at this number?"

"Anytime, day or night," he practically purred, making her want to reach through the line and punch him.

"I'll be in touch when I have something." She disconnected before he could respond and met Jay's gaze.

Once again his look was hard, unreadable. "You did good," he murmured before standing. As he did, Vadim, Wyatt and Hayden all stood. She just wanted to hide now that her past with Kevin had officially been exposed to people she admired. Jay looked down at her. "I'll be back later, but Iris will be here with you and we'll have two guards stationed outside and four waiting across the hall."

She wanted to ask him more questions, but knew now wasn't the time. Instead she merely nodded and watched as he silently left with the other men.

CHAPTER NINE

"Not that I'm not appreciative, but why didn't you go with them?" Ellie asked Iris. She knew the Serafina's head of security was very hands-on with anything security related to Wyatt or the hotel. And Ellie figured this counted in a big way.

Iris shrugged as she watched her carefully. Ellie felt like she was under a microscope as the tall, slender woman answered. "Wyatt will fill me in on everything, and...he wanted me to stay and check up on you. He didn't want you to be alone right now and he knew Jay was too stubborn to sit this out."

Surprise must have shown on Ellie's face, because Iris continued. "You shouldn't be surprised that Wyatt and the team care about you. You're more than just an employee."

Ellie swallowed hard. "I feel like a fraud half the time." Saying the words out loud felt freeing and terrifying at the same time. She'd grown up with practically nothing and while she might not have had her sister's talent, she'd been driven enough to graduate with honors and make something of her life. None of that made up for the fact that some days when she looked in the mirror she felt like she was playing dress up. Like the expensive shoes she bought herself or the nice makeup were all things to cover up who she truly was. A girl from the wrong side of the tracks.

"You know Wyatt and I grew up together?" Iris asked.

Ellie couldn't believe what she'd admitted out loud to the other woman in the first place so she welcomed the change in subject. "Yeah." That was pretty much all she knew though. Her boss was very private, especially when it concerned Iris.

"Did you know he was dirt poor because his alcoholic father blew every dime on whiskey?" Iris let out a surprisingly savage curse about the man Ellie knew was dead.

She shook her head. "No. I knew he grew up with very little because of that interview last year." A business magazine had done a feature on Wyatt because of how far he'd come. From a small, Georgia town not even on the map, he now owned real estate all over the globe and was a billionaire with a virtual empire.

"Well, poor is probably an understatement. People in town called him white trash and they called me a lot worse. My mom and I were the only Native Americans living in that backwoods place and considering my mom latched on to any man who would pay her bills, you can imagine what they called me and her." Iris let out a bitter laugh.

Ellie wasn't sure how she should respond or if she should. "I...had no idea."

Iris shrugged. "I don't generally talk about my past and you know Wyatt doesn't either, but it's not a secret. I'm not ashamed of where I came from. It doesn't define who I am." Those dark, knowing eyes probed Ellie's and it belatedly registered why Iris was telling her all this.

Ellie held the other woman's gaze, stunned by the personal revelations. "I understand what you're saying." And she wanted to get to that place where she didn't care about her past, didn't care what people thought when they looked at her. The truth was, she didn't have anything to prove to anyone. She just had to convince her brain of that.

Iris started to respond when the sound of the suite door opening made them both pause. Iris held a finger to her lips as she silently stood and withdrew a weapon from the back of her black pants. She moved to the edge of the hallway that led to the entryway then peered around. Immediately she relaxed and turned back to Ellie with a grin. "No threat."

A moment later Sierra rounded the corner of the hallway with a pastry box in her hand. Ellie really hoped there was chocolate in there. Sierra handed the box to Iris and made a beeline for Ellie. By the time she'd stood, the sweet chef was pulling her into a hug. "I'm so glad you're all right. I can't believe someone blew up your car."

Ellie hugged her back, not realizing how much she'd needed it until now. She'd come to adore Sierra in the short time the woman had been with Hayden, but she'd already liked her long before that. "I'm okay. Well, good enough," she said as they pulled apart. She couldn't say she was fine when someone was threatening her and those she cared for.

Sierra grinned and turned back to Iris who'd already opened the white box and was eyeing the contents hungrily. "If Iris hasn't eaten everything I've got some treats that will make you feel better."

"Sounds good to me. Maybe we can get into some of that wine?" Ellie nodded hopefully toward the marble-topped bar near one of the covered windows. There were bottles and bottles of expensive stuff and Ellie wasn't ashamed to admit she could use a little vino to take the edge off her nerves.

"None for me because I'm on duty, but you two have at it. Definitely on the hotel," Iris said. Then as an afterthought she said, "But that means I get more snacks."

Ellie laughed, the feeling bubbling up in her chest strange yet freeing. She'd been so worried that Iris and Sierra would judge her or look at her differently because of her past and now that she knew that wasn't true, she felt almost liberated.

Hours later, Ellie said goodbye to Sierra and Iris—who had a security issue that simply couldn't wait—and headed for the large bedroom. No word from Jay yet, but the suite was still being guarded and Sierra had a personal security guy escorting her home until Hayden could break away from whatever it was he was doing with Jay and the others.

Though Ellie wanted to stay up and wait for Jay she was emotionally exhausted and knew she needed to be on her game the next couple days. Whatever plan they were putting into motion she had no doubt it would affect everyone and she wanted to be ready. After stripping off her clothes she didn't bother digging through her suitcase as she climbed into bed and pulled the covers up to her neck. Barely a minute passed before she let sleep pull her under.

Jay leaned back against the cushioned swivel chair as Vadim dimmed the lights of the unused conference room they were all in. Right now the team for this was small; him, V, Wyatt and Hayden. Jay knew it would get bigger once things were in motion but for now it eased his mind that the group was small and one he trusted implicitly.

Angling his laptop—that looked as if it had the capability to launch a shuttle—toward one of the blank white walls, V plugged a small device into the back of the computer, hit a few buttons, then smiled in that tiger-like way of his as a 3D image projected into the unhindered space. It wasn't projected onto the wall but Jay understood why he'd needed the blank background.

The Serafina popped up, the entire building a skeleton of blue lines, showing nothing of the architectural genius that had gone into creating the hotel.

"Hold on," V murmured as he typed in commands. A moment later the blueprint of the whole building fell away as he zoomed in on a room in the second level of the hotel. The room where the Dragon Collection was.

A moment later the outline of a display case appeared. That wasn't part of the actual architectural plans, but Jay knew V had added it for their purposes.

"As you all know, this room is basically impenetrable because of these security additions." He sounded smug, likely because some of them had been his idea. "Even if someone wants to come in through the vents, the alarm will be triggered. This case," he marked it with his laser pointer, "is even protected underneath on the slim chance someone tries to come up from the floor below. The entire ceiling of that floor is rigged with sensors."

"V, we know all this." Wyatt sounded mildly impatient, a much more subdued version of what Jay was feeling.

He wanted to get to the damn point so he could get back to Ellie. She'd looked so lost and embarrassed as she called her ex and when he'd called her baby, Jay had seen red. But she'd done well. Now it was up to them to bring this guy down. Jay just wanted to end the asshole's life, but knew that wasn't the right way.

V let out an exasperated sigh and looked at Wyatt, those pale eyes seeming to glow in the dim lighting from the 3D display. "Would you like to do the presentation?"

Wyatt just rolled his eyes. For some reason he allowed V to talk to him—and anyone except Iris—the way he wanted. V was never overtly rude, just…lacked certain social skills. "No, but I'd like to get out of here sometime before midnight and I know Jay wants to get back to Ellie. She's scared, V."

At that Vadim's expression softened. "Yes, of course. Sorry." He turned back to the hologram. "All these sensors are shown on the building plans." He pointed to the main ones near the doors and in the vents. "But these were installed afterward and I made sure there is no trace of this final plan anywhere."

"What's in the floor directly beneath the display?" Unlike Hayden and V, Jay didn't work directly at the Serafina except when needed. He was Wyatt's go-to guy for pretty much everything in addition to his personal guard, but he didn't have the knowledge of the hotel like they did.

"Nothing until the end of the month," Wyatt said.

"If it's empty..." Jay trailed off and the others nodded.

"Yes. This will be the only way for Kevin Murrell and his men to take the jewels. The room is also guarded 24/7 in case anyone gets ideas, but they don't know that and we will remove the guards in the time leading up to their robbery."

"So Ellie will give him altered plans and unless he's a complete idiot, he'll make the choice we want him to make and go through the first floor ceiling. What about a visual?" Jay asked.

"We already have cameras installed in the display room and in the room below," Hayden said. "And during the time of the robbery we'll have an extra team standing nearby. Not to mention they'll be taking replicas anyway."

Jay nodded, already figuring that was the case. He knew Wyatt had them made as soon as he'd agreed to showcase the real jewels. The replicas were backups for situations just like this. Thank God the man was always prepared. "What happens after they take the replica jewels?" Jay wanted Kevin brought down, and that would be easily done once the idiot took what he thought was the real Dragon Collection, but he wasn't sure what Wyatt wanted.

"We let him leave. The second he clears the building we sound the alarm, as if our team has just discovered the breach. Then we let him meet with his boss, who I'm assuming will be De Luca," Wyatt said, all confidence.

"Then?"

"Then...let me worry about that."

Jay gave him a hard look, annoyed at Wyatt's lack of disclosure. That wasn't like him to hold back, not from Jay. "Really?"

Wyatt sighed. "I'm not withholding. I need to make a couple calls before we go any further, but I like this plan. No matter what he's not getting the real jewels. I'm keeping them locked in one of the vaults from now until he's arrested. But I want De Luca removed from Vegas permanently and I may have a way to make that happen. For now, we just need Ellie to give these plans to Murrell. It sounds like he's meeting with De Luca on Monday. Or whoever wants him to do this."

"It can't seem too easy. She can give them to him Sunday night. Make the bastard sweat," Jay muttered.

Wyatt nodded. "Agreed. I've got some media thing to deal with tomorrow..." Trailing off, he glanced at his watch. "Today. I want Ellie with us, otherwise it will seem odd. It's got to seem like everything is normal with all of us."

Jay gritted his teeth, but nodded. If Ellie suddenly disappeared for a couple days it would be obvious that she was under lockdown or in hiding. And that would bring up too many questions from Murrell. It had to appear like she was still working and living her life like normal. "I'll beef up our security team." The only reason he was agreeing was because the event was a low-key Q&A in a private room that no one other than the pre-approved media personnel would have access to. And he'd already vetted everyone coming—and knew most of them from past events.

"I have no doubt you will." Wyatt stood, looking exhausted and Jay felt a twinge of guilt that his boss was being pulled into this when he had so many other responsibilities. "Now go see Ellie."

Jay didn't need to be told twice. If Wyatt said he'd keep him in the loop, Jay had no doubt he would. Even if that meant a call at three in the morning. "Thanks."

Hayden nodded at the others before walking out with Jay. His brother clapped him lightly on the shoulder. "We're going to keep your girl safe."

"Yeah." That was definitely a concern, but Jay was more worried about their future and what Ellie wanted from him. He'd told her the ball was in her court and that scared the hell out of him. What if she… He mentally shook himself when he realized his brother was saying something else. "What?"

Hayden chuckled as he looked at the screen of his phone. "Our ladies got a little tipsy tonight. Sierra left me some interesting texts."

Despite his dark mood, Jay grinned. He loved seeing his brother so happy. Unlike him, Hayden had left the Navy because of an injury. His brother hadn't been ready to leave the Teams and Sierra had brought him out of his year-long surliness. She'd reached him in a way no one else had been able to. "Get home to her. I'm heading upstairs now."

After a brief hug, his brother left and Jay made his way to the private elevators. They were on the security floor so he'd be able to bypass seeing anyone. Which was good because he didn't feel up to making small talk. Jay checked his phone and had a couple texts including one from Iris telling him she'd had to leave Ellie, but that the guards on duty were the best.

Once he made it up to their floor he saw that Iris had been serious. She must have called in a different team or maybe they'd had a shift change because Logan and Roman MacNeil were standing guard. The twin brothers were both former Marines, both highly trained and not part of the normal hotel security detail. Like him, they were part of Wyatt's personal detail. And they were damn good at what they did.

"Hey you fucking jarheads," he said as he neared them.

They looked like sentries standing guard. Roman didn't crack a smile, but Logan did. "Whatever squid." He glanced at the closed door then back at Jay, his expression turning as serious as his brother's. "What's going on? Are you and Ellie in some kind of trouble?"

He ignored the questions because he couldn't answer them. "Have you talked to her?"

Logan nodded. "Briefly when she said goodbye to Sierra. She told us she was going to bed and she looked…I don't know, not like her normal self. Just wanted to make sure everything's cool."

"I can't talk about what's going on just yet, but I'll fill you in as soon as I can. It goes without saying that us staying here under guard isn't common knowledge and isn't to be shared." Jay figured Iris had already told them that, but wanted to reiterate it. Anything for Ellie's safety.

Roman snorted, his first reaction since Jay had arrived. He pinned him with that odd stare. It was easy to tell the twins apart because of Roman's different colored eyes. One brown and one blue-green that reminded Jay of the Pacific. "You know us better than that."

"Yeah, I do. Thanks for looking out." After another minute of bullshitting, he headed inside and nearly sagged against the front door before locking it.

Out of habit, he checked the entire suite before he made his way to the bedroom. The thick drapes had been opened about a foot, letting in some of the colorful nightlife. A thick ribbon of outside light streamed through, bathing the big bed and illuminating the top half of Ellie's very naked breasts.

Jay's body tightened with undeniable need. Damn it, he wanted her to make up her mind about them, to choose him, to trust him, before he buried himself inside her yet again. But it was impossible to show control around Ellie. The woman was his only drug of choice. Right now, he needed another fix.

CHAPTER TEN

Jay watched the steady rise and fall of Ellie's chest, wanting nothing more than to wake her up in one of the many erotic ways he'd done over the past year and some odd months they'd been together. His body ached to have her, to hold her, but...she needed sleep.

He stripped off everything but his slacks before slipping into bed next to her. Normally he slept naked too, but right now he didn't trust himself. Despite his size, the bed barely depressed underneath him as he moved in behind her.

Wrapping his arm around her compact body, he pulled her back tight against his chest, savoring the feel of her skin on his. She sighed in her sleep, softly murmuring his name and he fought a groan when she wiggled her backside against his hardening length. Was she trying to kill him?

Closing his eyes, he tried to force everything out of his mind so he could sleep. He'd had to do that too many times to count in the past. It was one of the many things that had been drilled into him as a SEAL. Eat whenever you could because you never knew when your next meal was coming. And catch Zs when you could because you never knew when you'd get to rest again. Normally his body listened to all his instructions. Throw Ellie into the mix, however, and he was screwed.

When she rolled over, mumbling something under her breath, and she slid her arm around his waist, burying her face against his neck and pressing her breasts against his chest, he knew that yes, she was definitely trying to kill him. He inhaled her sweet vanilla scent and found himself reminiscing about the first time they'd finally made love.

It had happened over a year ago and he still couldn't get enough of her...

He knocked on the hotel room door, tense and edgy as he waited for Ellie to answer. He'd wanted to surprise her, but now he was wondering why she wasn't answering the door. There was a snowstorm brewing so he didn't think she'd gone out.

The whole team had arrived in New York the night before for a deal Wyatt was working on. Wyatt, Iris and Ellie had been in meetings all day and Roman and Logan had been their personal detail because Wyatt had wanted Jay to take care of some personal things he didn't trust anyone else with. Supposedly.

Jay had only been back at work for a couple weeks and he wondered if Wyatt was still worried about him. Or worse, didn't think he was up to the job. He'd passed all his physicals and he was fine. His fractured ribs had taken a solid six weeks to heal because of the severity of his injury, but Wyatt had made him take another two weeks of bed rest. Which was just ridiculous. Then he'd made him take another two weeks off—just in case. Jay had been hurt worse than that in the Teams, something Wyatt knew. But his boss had been insane over Jay's injuries. Jay figured it was partially guilt since that bomb had been meant for him, but hell, that was Jay's damn job—protecting Wyatt.

Ellie had been just as bad. They'd started dating basically from the moment she'd walked into his hospital room back in Miami, but she'd been taking care of him and worrying over him worse than he'd imagined. He didn't want to be someone she took care of. And even though he'd been fine for weeks she was still putting the brakes on in the bedroom. Not because she didn't want him—because he could see the truth in her eyes when she looked at him—but because she thought of him as...hell if he knew. All he knew was that he wasn't an invalid and things were about to change.

Tonight.

He was going to take care of her in every way he'd been fantasizing about. He banged on the door again, frustration welling up inside him with each second that ticked by.

"Hold on," *Ellie snapped. A moment later the door flew open and the angry expression on her face melted away.* "Why are you banging on the door like a maniac? Is everything okay? Did you put a strain on yourself today?" *She glanced down at his mid-section, assessing him as she bit down on her bottom lip in clear concern.*

"I'm fine," he gritted out. "Why didn't you ask who it was? And why aren't you answering your phone?" He growled out the words, but immediately wanted to take them back. He hadn't come here to snap at her and he'd just let loose on her like a jackass.

"I..." She seemed stunned by his tone for a moment, but then she scowled at him. "This is a safe hotel, Jay. I don't need a lecture on security precautions. And I turned my phone to silent during our last meeting and forgot to turn it back on. It's been a long day." She crossed her arms over her chest and glared at him. She was wearing one of the plush white hotel robes. Normally she secured her hair into a twist at her nape, but now it fell around her face in soft, messy waves, making him want to run his hands through it as he claimed her mouth. Without heels on and no makeup, she looked adorable. And all his. Tonight he planned to show her just how much he wanted her.

He scrubbed a hand over his face. "I didn't mean to snap, sorry. I just missed you."

All the steam left her as she let her arms drop. She reached for him, then paused, as if afraid to hurt him. He nearly snorted at the thought. He outweighed her by God only knew how much and she was barely a couple inches over five feet. "I missed you too."

Her tentativeness drove him crazy. Especially when he was fine. More than fine. "Can I come in?"

"Of course." *She nodded, her dark eyes flaring with heat as she stepped back. But then it disappeared as she eyed him in that critical way he was coming to loathe.* "How are you feeling?" *she asked as he shut the door behind them.* "I can't believe Wyatt had you running errands."

The slight tether he had on his emotions slipped. "Take off your robe."

Her eyes widened, confusion and lust mixing together. "What?"

"Robe. Off. I want to see you." *Did he ever. So bad he ached for just a look, just a touch.*

She twined her fingers around the securely tied belt. "Jay... Are you sure?"

"It's been twelve weeks, Ellie. Twelve. Weeks." *He was barely hanging onto his control at this point.* "I was healed six weeks ago. I understand and appreciate everyone's concern, but it's not necessary. Do you not want me? Is that the issue?" *He knew it wasn't, or he hoped it wasn't. A small thread of fear slid through him after he asked the question.*

She rolled her eyes, easing that fear immediately. "Of course I want you, it's just—"

"Then I want to see you. Now." *He knew he was being highhanded, but in the bedroom, he liked to dominate. Not with ropes or anything—though the thought of binding Ellie was hot—but he needed to be in control.*

Ellie's cheeks flushed pink, her eyes glittering with a raw hunger he hadn't seen since before the explosion. Her fingers shook as she pulled the tie free, letting the oversized robe fall open.

It parted, just exposing the expanse of skin between the soft swell of her breasts. His gaze raked down the rest of her body, taking in the barest flash of her flat stomach. Unfortunately lacy black underwear covered what he wanted to see most.

"All the way off," he managed to rasp out.

"Sure you can handle that?" she asked, pure seduction in her voice.

His gaze snapped to hers and relief flooded him to see a hunger so potent it matched his own glittering there. Oh yeah, they weren't making it to the bed. He had a better idea.

Before he could respond, she shrugged out of the robe, letting it pool around her feet. For a moment, she clenched her hands at her sides, as if restraining from covering herself.

Though he couldn't fathom why she'd ever want to. Her perfect pink nipples tightened under his scrutiny and it took restraint not to suck one into his mouth. Not yet. He wanted to drink his fill of her. Compact and curvy, he wanted to trace his fingers and mouth over every soft inch of her body. Starting now.

Without further thought, he went down on his knees in front of her. Grasping the delicate material, he tugged her panties down her legs then lightly pushed on her stomach moving them until her back hit the wall. She made a little gasping sound, but didn't protest.

He looked up at her, pinning her gaze with his. "Put your leg over my shoulder."

Her mouth parted, her breathing coming in ragged as she did what he said.

As he looked at her parted, wet folds, his cock pushed even harder against his pants. He wanted to push deep inside her, but needed to taste her more. "Are you already wet for me?" he whispered, blowing softly against her.

She let out a nonsensical sound. Her heel dug into his back as she rolled her hips once, barely coming in contact with his face.

He flicked his tongue out, teasing her clit with the barest hint of pressure.

"I was thinking about you before you showed up at my door." The words came out in a rush, as if it was a confession.

Her words shattered through him as he imagined her elegant fingers pushing into her tight sheath. Swallowing hard, he looked up at her. She slid her fingers through his short hair, gripping his scalp.

"Did you touch yourself?" he demanded, hoping she had.

Breathing ragged, she shook her head. "Not yet."

His cock pulsed even harder, wanting to be freed. "Have you touched yourself before while thinking about me?"

Her face flamed crimson, but she nodded. His throat tightened, making it impossible for him to speak. She'd been so tentative around him the past twelve weeks, but to know she'd stroked herself while thinking of him... He buried his face between her legs. The need to have her on his tongue was overwhelming.

She groaned, her fingers digging into his head as she rolled her hips against his face. The little moans and sounds she made as he tasted and teased her drove him insane. Wanting to push her over the edge so he could bury himself inside her, he tested her slickness with one finger.

Though tight, her body welcomed him, her back arching away from the wall. Oh yeah, she was like an explosive, ready to go off at any moment. God, how he wanted to taste her release when she did.

Knowing how wet she was for him, that she wanted this as much as he wanted her, he groaned against her swollen clit and increased his pressure. The harder he stroked her, the harsher her breathing grew, the more her body shook and the tighter she gripped his head. As if she was afraid he'd stop. No way in hell was that happening.

He pushed a second finger in her and felt her inner walls tighten convulsively. She was so damn close he could feel it. Dragging his fingers in and out of her, he smiled against her slick folds when he realized he'd hit the perfect rhythm. Not too fast, not too slow, and he slightly curved his fingers each time he hit that sensitive spot that made her jerk against him.

"Jay..." Faster than he'd expected, she surged into climax, her body bowing tight as her heel dug into his back even hard-

er. Her slickness covered his fingers as her orgasm flowed, seeming to go on forever until she lessened her grip on his head and let her leg go lax.

With his two fingers still buried deep inside her, he savored the way her inner walls continued to clench around him in sporadic little bursts. Looking up at Ellie, he saw that her eyes were closed and a small smile played against her slightly parted lips.

She looked satisfied. Sated. And definitely all his.

Claiming her was a need growing inside him. As he stood, he withdrew his fingers but cupped her mound.

Her eyes opened as he moved, but they remained heavy-lidded as she placed her palms on his bare chest. "That was amazing." Her voice was raspy, unsteady and so very un-Ellie like.

"We're just getting started," he murmured before capturing her mouth with his.

She immediately wrapped her arms around him, linking her fingers behind his neck as she pressed her breasts to his chest. He could feel the outline of her hardened nipples, but he wanted that skin to skin contact. Wanted to feel every inch of her against him.

Grabbing her hips, he jerked her to him before hoisting her up. She let out a yelp of surprise, but wrapped her legs around him and continued teasing her tongue against his. Each flick of her tongue had him wondering what it would feel like to have her lips wrapped around his cock.

But not yet. Not until he'd had his fill of her. Some days he wondered if that was even possible.

He walked them into the dimly lit bathroom, grateful the counter was uncluttered as he set her on the edge of it. Keeping his gaze locked on hers, he started stripping. First his tie, then his jacket and next his shirt. Dark eyes glinting with fire, she went to undo his belt, but he stopped her. He felt like a randy teenager and wanted to be inside her when he came. Not her damn hand. Weeks ago they'd been tested and she was already on the Pill so there was nothing holding him back from feeling every sweet inch of her.

Once he was completely naked Ellie's eyes widened when they landed on his erection. Pure pleasure punched through him as she smiled and stroked him once. When she squeezed ever so lightly, he thought he might have a heart attack.

"Ellie." All he could get out was her name. Anything else was too much effort.

Her gaze met his, the fire burning there scorching him. Without a word he clasped her hips and slid her off the counter. She was pliant as she let him turn her around to face the mirror. Taking him by surprise, she lifted her ass slightly and spread her legs a little farther apart.

Slowly, he ran a hand over her soft backside, loving the feel of her smooth skin.

"Don't make me wait," she whispered.

Not trusting his voice, he nodded and guided himself to her slick entrance. The second he pushed deep inside her, his entire body pulled taut, all his muscles straining under the raw sensation of having her molded around his hard length. It was heaven and hell.

"Jay," Ellie murmured. Her body shifted against his and his eyes flew open.

He'd started thinking about their first time and must have dozed as he fantasized. Blinking, he looked down to find her still sleeping. She mumbled his name again as her fingers tightened against his chest and she burrowed closer to him. Even though she didn't say much, a tremble snaked through her, making him think she was scared or having a bad dream.

"I'm right here, baby," he whispered, thankful when she immediately stilled against him. He was right where he wanted to be and he wasn't going anywhere. Not unless she told him to.

CHAPTER ELEVEN

Ellie opened her eyes with a start but immediately relaxed as she realized she was in the secure hotel suite at the Serafina. But Jay wasn't in bed with her. A low grade panic hummed through her as she glanced around the room to find it empty. The door to the adjoining bathroom was open and the light was off so Jay wasn't in there. But the spot next to her on the bed was depressed, as was the pillow so Jay had been here. She'd been so wiped out she didn't even remember him coming in last night.

Sliding out of bed, she snagged one of the room robes Jay must have left out for her and slipped it on. As she tightened the belt, she stepped out into the main room to find Roman MacNeil rolling in a room service tray. The only reason she knew it was Roman was because of his different colored eyes.

He half-smiled as he pushed it into the living room area. "Hey, Ellie. Jay had this sent up, said you'd be waking up soon."

Ellie smiled to herself. Jay definitely knew her. It didn't seem to matter that she'd had the most emotionally taxing day yesterday, her car had been blown up and she'd had more wine than she should have with Sierra, she still woke up at five-thirty in the morning like clockwork. "Thanks. Where's Jay?"

"He dipped out of here about twenty minutes ago. Didn't say why, just that me and Logan better take care of you or lose some very important body parts." The normally stoic former-Marine cracked another smile, taking her by surprise. "Do you want me to open the drapes for you?"

She blinked at the question and shook her head. "No, but thank you. You don't need to do anything else. I appreciate the breakfast." If she had to guess there was a bowl of fruit under the silver dome and possibly some Greek yogurt. Her favorite breakfast. Something Jay knew because she had it practically every morning. Next to the plate-covered dome was an elegant silver coffee carafe. Her mouth watered at the thought of the steaming hot liquid of beauty. Whoever had discovered coffee was a genius.

"You sure? Jay was pretty intent about us making sure you were okay. And I value all my body parts." His expression was deadpan now—the Roman she knew.

Still grinning, she nodded. "I'm sure. Did Jay say anything else?"

"Just that when you were ready we were to escort you down to your office and that we'll be with you and Wyatt most of the day."

Wyatt often had a security team guarding him, though that was usually on business trips. But it sounded like this team was for her. Which made her reality even scarier. She hated that Kevin had put her in this position, but knew there was nothing she could do about it. "After I eat it won't take me long to get ready, so I'll be out soon."

He nodded once. "We'll be waiting."

After he'd gone, she opened the dome and sure enough a colorful display of mixed fruit was there along with the yogurt. But there was also a small white envelope with her name on it. Curious, she opened it up and immediately smiled at the familiar bold script. It was from Jay. *You looked so peaceful, didn't want to wake you. We've got a full day and everything needs to look normal so head to work on schedule. I've got my phone on me. Call if you need anything or just want to talk. Love you.*

Feeling better than she had just hours ago, she tucked the note into the pocket of the robe. If they could just get through this mess, she wasn't letting Jay go. Not without a fight. Tonight she planned to show him exactly how much he meant to her.

Ellie nodded at Roman and Logan once they reached her office door. "You guys don't have to—"

"We are under strict instructions to shadow you all day," Logan said, usually the speaker of the two.

"Oh, ah, okay." She hadn't realized they'd actually be shadowing her. "Come on in then." She hadn't had a chance to talk to Wyatt one-on-one, but he hadn't been keen on letting her go so she hoped she still had a job and not just for the public image until this Kevin mess was settled. Once inside the big room, she motioned to the coffee station and lounge area. "Make yourselves comfortable."

Her office was attached to Wyatt's and she could hear him shouting next door. And it was only six-thirty in the morning. The noise level was unusual so she had a feeling she knew who he was talking to. Dropping her purse onto her seat, she didn't wait for a response before heading to the connecting door he almost always kept open. Since he'd gotten married, he'd more or less made his office at the Serafina his main base of operations. They'd moved offices a year ago, not long after the hotel had opened, and Ellie much more preferred this location. Probably because she was friends with so many of the staff.

When she paused in the doorway, Wyatt looked up from his desk, his expression dark. "I'll call you back," he gritted out before slamming the phone down. "That Brit drives me insane."

Ellie bit back a smile, knowing who he was referring to. Rhys Martin Maxwell IV, a man Wyatt had had business dealings with in the past, but usually they just tried to outbid each other at auctions. It was a strange, semi-friendly rivalry that Ellie didn't quite understand. "So this isn't business related then."

"Bastard said he was going to sell the painting to me, but this morning he changed his mind. Said since I'm already married to the most beautiful woman I didn't need any more beauty in my life. I want to throttle him."

Ellie laughed. "I don't know why you're surprised. He's never going to sell." The painting in question was a starkly beautiful image of the aurora borealis. Having seen it in person once, she could attest that it was truly breathtaking. It had been the very first thing the two men had bid on against each other. It had also been the birth of their rivalry and sort-of friendship. "If he does, I think it would be akin to admitting defeat in this weird rivalry you two have."

"Weird?"

"It's not normal, Wyatt." Now she didn't hide her grin.

Wyatt's expression softened as he leaned back in his custom-made ergonomic chair. "It's good to see you smile."

She wrapped her arms around herself as she stepped into his office. It was the first time she'd ever truly felt nervous around him. "Thank you. For everything. I can't tell you how much I appreciate you and Jay and everyone for…just thank you."

"You quit because you didn't want to be in a position to have to steal from me. That alone shows me how loyal you are, Ellie. I don't want your thanks. I just wish you'd come to me or more importantly, to Jay, instead of running."

She crossed the distance to his desk and sat on one of the ridiculously comfortable arm chairs. He was all about comfort and luxury. "I thought I was doing the right thing."

"I get it, maybe more than you think. But no more running. We're handling this and no one's going to bother you again." The underlying deadly threat in his voice sent a shiver up her spine, but it wasn't a surprise.

"So you weren't kidding about me still having a job? Even after Kevin is…out of the picture?" She knew Wyatt enough that she was sure he'd been serious when he spoke the words, but after everything he'd learned about her, she couldn't fight the insecurity battling inside her.

He snorted as if the question was ludicrous. Which made her feel a hundred times more secure. "You'll always have a job. And right now, we've got to get ready for today's appearance. My speech—"

"Is in your inbox." She'd sent it a week ago. "And I've already got a list of pre-approved questions. I'm sure you'll get a few surprises, but you'll be fine." He always was under pressure. In fact, he thrived on it.

"Good." Back to business, they spent the next ten minutes going over the rest of the day, down to the last detail.

Ellie was nervous about being in public after what had happened to her car, but she knew it was the only way to make things appear normal. It wasn't as if Kevin wanted her dead. At least not yet. Because she had no doubt he'd want to get rid of her after she got him what he wanted. Thankfully the idiot needed her alive for his ridiculous plan.

After finishing up with Wyatt she headed to her office. Roman and Logan stood when they saw her, but she shook her head. "I'm staying put for the next few hours so you two might get bored." The floor was secure, only accessible with the right key card and the security room had constant visual access outside their offices so she wasn't worried about a surprise attack or visit from anyone. Right now they were probably more secure than anywhere else in Vegas.

"Let us know if you need anything," Logan said before nodding at Roman. "We'll be standing guard outside."

"Thanks, I will." Once she had her office to herself, she got to work catching up on over a hundred emails, over two dozen phone calls around the world to various business interests of Wyatt's, and some tedious filing that needed to be done. Pretty soon she'd need an assistant of her own. Something she needed to talk to Wyatt about, but that could wait a few weeks.

Even as she embroiled herself in work, her mind was never far from thoughts of Jay. She was surprised he hadn't wanted to guard her himself, but she figured he was doing something toward their mysterious plan to bring Kevin down. Pulling out her cell phone, she texted him.

Thanks for having breakfast sent up. Wish you'd woken me last night.

A moment later, her phone pinged with a return text. *No prob. You looked like you needed sleep.*

She bit her bottom lip and eyed her phone. They didn't text much since they saw each other so often so she hoped he was up for a little text-flirting. *I needed you inside me more.*

There was a long pause this time. *Are you trying to kill me?*

She grinned at his response. *Right now I'm wearing that gray skirt suit you like so much.* The knee-length pencil skirt and matching tailored jacket were perfectly respectable, but every time she wore the skirt Jay couldn't get inside her fast enough. She had no idea why either. He just went crazy when she wore it, taking her as soon as they got home or in one instance in one of the hotel bathrooms he'd cleared out.

Jay: *You look like a naughty librarian in that thing.*

Ellie: *That's why you like it so much?*

Jay: *I thought you knew.*

Ellie: *Tonight I'll wear just the skirt and jacket.* Meaning no blouse, bra or panties underneath. Something she didn't need to spell out.

Jay: *You are trying to kill me.*

Ellie: *Too bad I've got guards today or we could do it in my office.*

Jay: *You'll pay for this teasing.*

Ellie: *I hope so.*

Jay: *Gotta run, xo*

Ellie: *K, xo*

She grinned at Jay's xo symbol. Yeah, he was definitely a man worth fighting for.

CHAPTER TWELVE

Ellie stood a couple feet back and to the side of Wyatt's podium as he was asked another question. This time it was about his fairly new marriage instead of the new property he'd recently bought—which was what the media questionnaire was supposed to be about today. Not Wyatt's personal life. The room went silent, the more seasoned reporters looking at the idiot newbie with pity.

Wyatt didn't mind making appearances and was very approachable about all things business. But no one asked him about Iris. It was an unwritten rule. His wife was off-limits as a topic. Always.

"Next question. Ridley?" Ellie said, ignoring the man who would soon find himself on Ellie's little black list of media personnel she didn't invite or allow at these things.

Thankfully Ridley didn't miss a beat as he asked about the potential revenue the city could expect with this newest construction effort. And neither did Wyatt as he answered.

Ellie glanced over at Jay, who was standing on the other side of Wyatt. Tall, imposing, he might as well have been carved from stone as he scanned the small crowd. Always in battle mode during these things. Which just made her want him even more. Something she shouldn't be thinking about right now. She saw that he'd increased the security today, but not so much that it would seem odd. Ellie had two guards on her and so did Wyatt, not including Jay. Plus there were a few of the hotel security members sitting among the crowd, blending in perfectly.

As everything started to wind down, relief threaded through Ellie. Wyatt had moved this meeting to the end of the day instead of its originally scheduled time right after noon, and her stomach had started to make low, growling noises because she'd missed lunch. Her cell buzzed in her pocket, indicating a text. Still on the clock and knowing the text could be important, she fished it out while Wyatt smoothly answered another question.

She swiped her finger across the screen, typing in her security code. As she read the incoming text, the bottom of her stomach dropped out. *Green is a good color on you. The clock is ticking, bitch. Get me what I want or that suit is dead.*

Ellie's muscles tightened as she tried to keep herself from shaking. She didn't care about the bitch comment or the time frame. The number wasn't the same as the one Kevin had been calling her from before, but she knew it was him. And he knew what color her blouse was. Even worse, she knew the 'suit' mention referred to Jay. Which meant Kevin had to be here.

But that was impossible.

Taking a calming breath, she scanned the crowd, looking at the familiar faces. When she didn't see him anywhere, she looked toward the back of the room but only saw security members. She had to think. Maybe he wasn't here. But then how would he know what she was wearing? She'd gone straight from the hotel suite to her office today, then after a full day of phone calls, emails and employee issues that simply couldn't wait, she'd come here with Wyatt and the security team. Jay had met them right outside the room, escorting them the rest of the way in.

Battling nerves, she turned around to make sure Logan and Roman were still behind her and caught Jay's gaze. Those electric green eyes of his missed nothing. They narrowed the tiniest fraction, but she knew she couldn't let him know anything was bothering her. Not in full view of everyone. Especially if Kevin was in the room. If he saw her signaling to Jay then he'd know she'd told someone about his threats. Then that monster would know something was up and she was lying to him.

Tucking her phone back into her jacket pocket, she gave Jay a half-smile before facing the crowd again. As soon as they were alone she'd tell him about the text, but she couldn't risk giving herself away before then.

Seconds after Wyatt answered the last question, two members of the team stepped up, surrounding him on each side. One of them murmured something to him and after a nod at her, Wyatt headed out one of the back doors of the room which would take him directly to a private parking garage. She was surprised Jay wasn't going with them.

"Why aren't you leaving with Wyatt?" she asked as he made his way across the raised podium toward her. Out of the corner of her eye she spotted two people waiting to talk to her. She held out a hand letting them know she'd be a moment.

"What's wrong?" he murmured, low enough for her ears only. "I saw your face when you looked at your phone. Did he text you?"

"Yes, but I can't talk about it now," she murmured, pasting a big smile on her face. She stood on tiptoe and brushed her lips against his. "Give me sixty seconds then drag me away."

One of his hands reached out and clenched around her hip in that possessive way of his she adored before he nodded and let her go. But she sensed him standing behind her as she approached the two waiting individuals.

Right on schedule Jay tapped her shoulder, no doubt exactly a minute later. He murmured something about a work emergency loud enough for the others to hear. She smiled apologetically and broke away then watched as Roman and Logan boxed her in from the front and back in perfect synch.

"Come on. We're getting you out of here." Jay's voice was low again.

Subtly trying to scan everyone's faces, Ellie fell in step with the security team as they exited the room. "Don't react, but someone texted me about the clock ticking down. A different number than before. He mentioned the color of my top, which means he might be watching. He also mentioned 'the suit' and I'm sure it was a reference to you, not Wyatt. He threatened you." Her hands balled into tight fists at the thought.

Ever the professional, Jay didn't miss a beat as they strode past a row of slot machines on their way to the main lobby. The dings and whirs barely registered, the typical casino sounds white noise to her now. But she wondered why they were coming to the lobby instead of back toward the private elevators.

"I'm going to kill him," Jay murmured, a half-smile on his face, as if nothing was wrong. But the deadliness rolling off him was very real.

She slid her hand through his arm as they walked. "Jay—"

"Forward the message to me and V. V will see what he can get from the number. Logan and Roman are going to escort you from the hotel. They'll drive around for a while before looping back and entering through the private garage. We don't want anyone to know you're staying here." Again, his voice was so low that no one could possibly hear but her.

Her fingers dug into his forearm. "What about you?" After that text she didn't want him out of her sight. She knew that he could take care of himself more than most, but the fear she felt for him had sunk its claws deep in her chest and wasn't letting up anytime soon.

"I've got some stuff to take care of but I'll be in the suite in a few hours." His tone was abrupt.

"Stuff?"

He didn't answer and she gritted her teeth.

"Are you going to expand on that?"

"No."

"Then maybe I won't be wearing my—"

He cut off what she'd been about to say with a searing kiss as they reached the valet area outside the main lobby. She nearly stumbled, clutching at his chest as he claimed her mouth. And that was what he was doing, no doubt about it. The kiss only lasted a few seconds and when he pulled back, he ran his lips along her jaw, up to her ear, nipping her lobe between his teeth.

"You better be wearing what you said. I've been thinking about that all day," he growled.

His demanding tone sent a shiver down her spine. "We'll see," she whispered, though they both knew that she would be. Even though she knew it might dispel the flirty mood, she grabbed his hand and said, "Be careful."

Expression serious, he nodded. "Always. You know I'd be with you if I could. Roman and Logan are the best."

"I know. We need to seem like it's business as usual." Keeping Jay out of harm's way was all that mattered so even though she wanted him with her, she understood the need for normalcy.

After giving low-spoken instructions to Roman, Jay waited until the three of them had gotten into the already waiting company SUV. As soon as they drove away from the hotel Ellie pulled out her cell phone and texted Sierra. She needed a little help with her seduction plan tonight and Sierra was the perfect person to help her. Ellie was even more determined to fix things with Jay, to show him exactly how much she loved him.

"Lost them," Tadeo muttered to Kevin as he slammed on the brakes to avoid ramming into the back of a Jeep.

Kevin's hand tightened on the arm rest. Ellie wasn't staying at her home, which was to be expected since her car had been bombed. He'd wondered how she'd explained that to the police, but according to De Luca, who had a source at the police station, she'd claimed to have no idea who could want to hurt her in her official statement. The police were chalking it up to gang violence or an attack meant as a threat to her boss. Both were wrong, but as long as she kept her mouth shut about him, he didn't care what she told them. "Those guys are good."

He figured they must be hotel security or maybe her boss's personal guards. And they were definitely armed. Kevin hadn't seen any weapons on either man, but it was in the way they walked, the way they carried themselves. Same with the suit Ellie was with. After seeing the giant guy move, Kevin wondered if there wasn't more to him than he'd originally thought. Christiansen wouldn't have anyone guarding him who wasn't trained. Unfortunately all De Luca had been able to find out about Jay Wentworth were some basic financial records and that he'd been in the Navy. But nothing about what he'd done while he'd been in. After seeing him in person, Kevin had noticed some tats peeking past one of the sleeves of his jacket. In his experience, typical suits didn't have tats.

"Not surprising. What do you want to do?" Tadeo asked.

"Head back to the hotel. I want to take some more pictures. We've still got half an hour before the display closes." Even though he was still waiting for the building plans from Ellie, he and Tadeo were doing as much recon as they could. So far they had the daytime guards' schedule down, but he knew there had to be a shift change sometime after hours. Unfortunately there was no way to find that out without a big risk of being exposed. The casino was open 24/7, but not the display area and they had no business being on that floor after a certain time. Sure, they could come up with an excuse, but it would make them memorable. Something he couldn't risk.

"You sure she'll come through?"

"Yeah." He sounded more confident than he felt, which was good. He had to keep up appearances for Tadeo. He might like the guy but Kevin couldn't let his guard down. Not when he knew Tadeo would always look out for number one. Not that he blamed him. It was the law of survival, something prison had grilled into him even more.

When the phone Tadeo had given him buzzed in his pocket, he glanced at the incoming text message and didn't hide his smile. "She's got what we need and will give it to me tomorrow. Wants to set up a meeting at a public place."

"She might have backup. That big guy doesn't seem like he'll let her out of his sight, especially not after that car bombing. Did you see those guards on her?"

"This'll be a good way to test if she's lying." He texted back with the location of a private park and a time.

Her response was immediate. *I'll give you the time and place tomorrow. You'll have fifteen minutes to meet me at the designated place.*

Her demanding attitude pissed him off, but she held the cards and clearly knew it. He might be threatening her, but he needed something from her. Once he got it though, it would be a different game. Forcing himself to remain calm, he texted her back. Soon he'd have to ditch this phone and the other burner he'd texted her with.

After he'd seen her entering that media event from the floor of the casino he'd waited until the room had been locked down to text her. He just wished he'd been able to see her expression when she'd received it and the mention of her shirt color. She'd probably thought he had a visual on her right then. Which was what he wanted.

Ellie needed to stay on her toes, to be worried that he was watching all the time. Her fear would keep her from doing anything stupid, like trying to double-cross him.

CHAPTER THIRTEEN

"She's safe in the suite. We both swept and secured it before letting her enter," Roman said the moment he picked up Jay's call.

"Thanks," Jay said, hating that he wasn't with Ellie right now. He was downstairs getting the room directly underneath the one that housed the Dragon Collection prepped for the would-be robbery, but it felt as if he was hundreds of miles from her.

She was in good hands though. The twins were better trained than anyone on the security team and the fact that Wyatt had been willing to give Ellie two of his best men said a lot. "What's she doing now?"

"Not sure. She kicked us out. Said unless someone came down from the roof and had a glass cutter, no one was getting in the room and she wanted privacy." Roman chuckled lightly. "She's right too. Wyatt had this floor built with security in mind."

"I know." He'd been there when his boss had gone over the extra design features with the architect. Plus he knew Ellie had one of his weapons with her. He wouldn't have left her unarmed even with guards.

"I'm pretty sure we were followed," Roman continued.

His heart rate increased a fraction, even though it wasn't totally unexpected. "How many?"

"I saw two vehicles, but I think the second was following the guys tailing us."

Jay frowned, but listened as Roman went over the details about both vehicles he'd spotted. As of now Roman and Logan just knew that there was an increased security threat and Ellie was a top priority. They were being vigilant and doing their job, but not asking more questions, something Jay was thankful for.

Jay had already heard from Ellie that she'd texted Kevin with vague meeting details for tomorrow. Which was something Jay couldn't even think about right now. He didn't want her anywhere near that piece of garbage, but the file she needed to give him was simply too big for email. They'd discussed using cloud storage via a file hosting system but it was still too risky that the information she was giving him could become public or even be accessed by an employee of the hosting system. So in-person it was.

Once they disconnected, Jay relayed everything to Vadim who'd already tracked down the phone Ellie had received the text from. A standard burner phone with no other incoming or outgoing calls. Basically useless for now. V was still keeping tabs on the other phone Kevin had called her from though. Whatever his relationship with the owner of the phone, Tadeo Bejar, they seemed to be decent enough friends from what V had been able to pull up on the two men.

Jay wanted a tail on Kevin 24/7 but knew that would be a stupid move. If the man got even a hint that he was being watched it could screw up their plans. And it would only have to be one small thing to tip him off. He couldn't risk Ellie getting hurt.

"Check this out." V held out his laptop to Jay.

Taking the laptop, he eyed the screen, watching himself and V on the live feed. They were sitting in the middle of the empty room directly underneath the display case for the Dragon Collection—which was being replaced with fake jewels as they spoke. Wyatt was going to put the real ones in one of the vaults and he and Iris would be the only ones who knew exactly where they were.

"Tell me what I'm looking at," Jay said.

"Hold on." He reached over and tapped a button.

On screen, a small light green crisscross pattern covered the entire ceiling. Jay looked up and saw nothing. "The invisible sensors?"

"Yes. I made the openings tighter and I've linked the silent alarm to send alerts to all of our phones." Meaning, him, V, Wyatt, Iris and Hayden. In a couple hours Wyatt would be filling Roman and Logan in on everything but for now they were keeping everything close to the chest. "And after tomorrow I'll temporarily disable the alert to the police station."

"Wyatt's orders?" Jay asked. It was against the insurance company's requirements. The police alert had to be live at all times so in the event the jewels were stolen, they would be covered by the company.

"Yeah, if a call goes out over the radio, Wyatt doesn't want anyone listening to scanners picking up a message."

Jay nodded. They had the robbery part ironed out, but Wyatt was still working out the logistics of coordinating with the police. And his boss was being very quiet about everything, though they were supposed to get the final details tonight. "You done in here?" Jay asked, handing the laptop back to him.

"Yeah." He stood and Jay followed suit. "Let's head to the security room. I should have gotten some hits by now."

Jay knew he was talking about the facial recognition software the casino used to weed out people who'd been banned, or for other potential serious threats. V had plugged in Kevin and Tadeo's pictures earlier so if they'd been in or on the premises recently, the team would know soon enough.

Upstairs in V's office, Jay and the others all stood in front of the four screens on the wall. Each of the security team with management titles had something similar in their office.

"You're sure that's him?" Iris asked, eying the video critically.

Vadim nodded, his expression stoic. "Yeah. I got sixty percent of his face and the ears are right. It's a high statistical improbability that the computer screws up those measurements."

A man wearing a baseball cap, jeans and a long-sleeved T-shirt stood in front of a slot machine, almost absently pulling on the lever as he watched the nearby elevators. He kept his face angled down, as if he didn't want to be seen by any cameras. And he must know there were a ton of them considering he was in a casino.

Jay tensed as he watched Ellie exit the elevator with Roman and Logan surrounding her. It didn't matter that this was a recording, he hated that her ex was anywhere near her after what he'd done. The car bombing wasn't an idle threat. Wyatt was behind her with his team, but the man never took his eyes off Ellie, watching her head toward where Jay had been waiting for her earlier this afternoon.

"And I've got a couple more clips of him," V interrupted Jay's rage-fueled thoughts that Murrell had been so damn close to Ellie.

So close and Jay hadn't even realized.

On one of the other screens, a recorded feed of the showroom for the Dragon Collection appeared. The place was busy, people milling in and out and sure enough, Kevin was there. "He's taking pictures," Jay muttered.

"Yeah but so is everyone else," Iris said. "He's acting like a perfect tourist."

"When was this?" Jay asked.

"An hour before the shot with Ellie." He paused the feed, then pointed his controller at another screen. "And this is right after Ellie leaves with Roman and Logan." There was a clear shot of him getting into a minivan, but the windows were tinted, not giving them a visual of the driver.

"I bet it's his buddy, Tadeo. You get the license plate?" Hayden sounded as annoyed as Jay felt.

"Yep." V sounded smug. "There's no such license plate."

"As in the numbers don't exist in any system?" Wyatt asked.

V nodded. "They probably took two halves of different plates, then welded them together."

"Smart, impossible to trace so even if the vehicle is stolen we wouldn't know where to start looking," Jay said. Vadim shouldn't even have access to DMV records but he wasn't going to ask how the man knew the license plate didn't exist. If he didn't know, it gave him plausible deniability.

"What's interesting is this vehicle..." V trailed off as he zoomed in on a dark truck that pulled away after the minivan. "I was able to track them for a couple miles by hacking into CCTVs and this truck was definitely tailing them. I ran the plate and it exists, but I couldn't find out any details about the owner which tells me it might be a government vehicle."

"It is," Wyatt said, causing all eyes to turn to him. Even Iris looked surprised.

"How do you know?" she asked.

"Because I know the driver. I couldn't say anything until I was certain we were good to go, but remember Cody from the strip club?" Wyatt asked, looking at Jay.

Jay nodded.

"His full name is Cody Hurley and he's a detective. He doesn't normally do undercover work, but the job at Teaser's was part of his cover for...something. I don't know what. I just know it's over now and he's back at work. He and another detective—who I trust—know about what's going on and what we're planning. As soon as Ellie makes the drop to Murrell, he's going to have the SWAT team on standby indefinitely. They want to bring down De Luca in the worst way and with Murrell's link to him, they're foaming at the mouth for the chance. Unfortunately they think De Luca might have a contact in the department. No one high level, but with enough knowledge that De Luca's avoided prosecution too many times. It's the only reason Hurley is sitting on this. It's also why I'm having the police alert turned off. Hurley will be contacted directly by one of us in this room when everything goes down." He looked around at all of them. "After Murrell and his team leave with the jewels, the plan is for SWAT to infiltrate the meet for the Dragon Collection."

"Are we putting a tracker on the fakes?" Jay asked.

Wyatt shook his head. "No. I don't know how they know, but apparently Hurley says they'll make it to the meet place even if they lose Kevin and his crew. If I had to guess, I'd say he has a CI or something working for him, but frankly, I don't care. Even if the worst case scenario happens and Murrell gets away with the jewels, they're fake. De Luca will probably kill him for that alone. Which gets rid of Ellie's problem."

Jay nodded slowly, absorbing everything. It made sense that Hurley had a CI—a confidential informant—or he might even have an actual inside man. If the plan didn't work and Murrell realized that the jewels were a fake *before* meeting with De Luca then Murrell would know or at least suspect that Ellie had set him up. If that happened, Jay would deal with the problem then. "Do the police know everything we know? Everything V has done to get information on Murrell and Bejar?" Even though he thought he knew the answer, Jay asked anyway.

Iris snorted at the same time Wyatt shook his head. "They know what they need to know. At this point Hurley knows that we have a credible threat against the Dragon Collection. I told him it's a tip we received from a concerned citizen in exchange for compensation. If all goes well he's going to get credit for bringing down De Luca and the SWAT team will publicly get the accolades they deserve. It's a win-win for them. If Hurley knows more, he'd have to disclose it."

So he wasn't asking questions. Jay liked that. "All this sounds good. Ellie still needs to set up the drop-off location for tomorrow and we'll need to go over the location and pinpoint exactly where everyone will be, but we can do that in the morning. I need to relieve the twins anyway because I want them with us tomorrow. Should I send them down here?" he asked Iris.

She nodded. "Yeah, I'll brief them on everything."

"Take this with you if you have a chance for some light reading." V handed him a binder with information on Murrell and Bejar, no doubt.

At this point Jay didn't care, but he took it. He would read it in the morning because something told him he wouldn't have a chance to tonight. He just wanted to get to Ellie. Especially if she planned to wear what she'd promised. Shoving that thought aside for now, he spoke to his brother for a few minutes in private before heading upstairs. He texted Ellie to let her know he was on his way up and she told him to meet her on the balcony. It was private and they were so high up that it would be damn near impossible for anyone to get to her, but still, he didn't like her outside. He didn't like anything about this entire damn situation.

Even though he told himself to hold off reading the file, he flipped it open as the elevator ascended. As he scanned the basics on Murrell, he could feel his anger ratcheting up so he snapped it shut when the doors whooshed open on their floor.

After stepping out he immediately spotted the twins and two other members of his team waiting outside the suite door. Good, they were ready for a shift change which meant he didn't have to call them in as replacements. This was why he was selective about his hires. He needed people who knew what needed to be done and did it without being told. Jay nodded at everyone. "Roman, Logan, head down to the security floor. Iris needs to go over some stuff with you. And get some sleep tonight. We need you alert tomorrow."

He knew they must have questions, but professionals that they were, they just nodded and headed for the elevators without even a crack about him being a squid. After he talked with the other team members for a few seconds, he headed inside.

Soft music filtered in from somewhere and there were flameless battery-operated candles everywhere. Some he recognized from their home and wondered how the hell she'd gotten them here. Since she'd said she was on the balcony, he dropped the file on the nearest couch and made his way to the open French doors. The sheer white curtains billowed softly, flapping open to reveal even more flameless candles on one of the decorative mosaic tables outside.

As he stepped outside, he froze. Ellie was stretched out on one of the cushioned lounge chairs, wearing exactly what she'd said she would. With just a jacket and that skirt he loved to hike up to her hips, she was his walking wet dream. The jacket was unbuttoned but still covered her breasts, only giving him a flash of skin. She was also wearing wire-rimmed glasses he knew she didn't need and had piled her hair on top of her head in a messy bun.

Smiling seductively, she pushed up from the seat, her four inch heels clicking against the stone. "Can I help you check out a book?" she asked, her voice pure sex and sin as she took on the naughty librarian role.

Jay's tongue stuck to the roof of his mouth as he tried to formulate an answer, but his mind went completely blank at the erotic sight.

CHAPTER FOURTEEN

Ellie couldn't remember ever being so nervous around Jay. Their first time together had been intense and hot and not much had changed since then. But they'd never done any sort of role playing or dressing up. She wasn't sure if this counted, but when he'd mentioned envisioning her as a naughty librarian she'd decided to go all out. Thankfully Sierra had been able to snag some costume glasses for her from one of the casino shows.

If the hungry expression on Jay's face was any indication, Ellie's look was perfect. He seemed almost frozen to the spot. His tie was loosened sexily around his neck, his top button opened and his jacket was perfectly rumpled.

It was a little chilly so high up, but she didn't care. Striding up to him, she watched as he visibly swallowed, his heated gaze raking over her from head to toe. When he landed on the bare expanse of her stomach and in between her covered breasts, that gaze went molten. As soon as she was within touching distance, he reached for her but she swatted his hands away.

"No touching until I say."

He blinked and she could see that dominant streak of his flare to life. She ignored it. Tonight she just wanted to take care of him. He was always so giving in and out of the bedroom and after the way he'd stepped up to protect her, not caring about the danger he was putting himself in, she wanted to show him how much he meant to her. Words would only get her so far. Actions were better. At least he listened and kept his hands at his sides.

With her heels, she had more of a height advantage than usual. Reaching up, she slid her fingers under the shoulders of his jacket and pulled it off.

"What are you doing?" Jay murmured.

As if he didn't know. "Exactly what I want and what you need," she said as she tossed the jacket onto the nearest chair. Next she worked his tie off, then his button-down shirt until all that expanse of gorgeous, taut muscular skin was bared to her. Her mouth practically watered as she drank him in.

When he reached for her again, once more she swatted at his hands. He blinked in surprise, making her grin.

"I told you no touching. Now lay back there." She pointed to the lounge chair she'd been on when he arrived.

The tendons in his arms tightened and flexed and she knew he was fighting that dominant urge he always displayed in the bedroom. She loved everything about his need to possess her between the sheets—or on the floor and in the shower—but she wanted to show him how much she cared for him. Something told her he wouldn't let her do this for long so she was taking advantage of his compliance.

When he sat on the edge of the lounge chair, she pointed. "Back farther. Stretch out."

"You're very demanding tonight." His tone was a mix of heat and a little confusion.

He rarely let her take charge in the bedroom and that worked wonderfully for their relationship, but this role reversal was fun. She knew he wasn't completely comfortable giving up control, so she hoped he trusted her enough to give him what he needed. Thankfully he did what she said and stretched out so that he was reclining.

Slowly she approached him, loving the hunger in his eyes, loving that it was all for her. First she took off her glasses, grinning when he swallowed audibly. Then she reached around her back and slowly tugged down the zipper of her skirt. His eyes went molten as he watched her. Moving intentionally slow, she pushed the skirt over her hips, letting it pool around her feet soundlessly. Tracking every movement, he made a strangled sound when she was bared to him.

Straddling him, she scooted down until she slid over his covered erection. He shuddered and this time he ignored her rules, touching her as he put his hands on her hips. His fingers clenched possessively. "You're a wet dream come to life," he rasped out as he rolled his hips once, his hard length rubbing against her already pulsing clit.

Having Jay like this was making her impossibly turned on. It didn't matter how many times she'd seen him naked, having him stretched out like this and all for her...her inner walls clenched, empty and needing to be filled by him. But first she wanted to taste him, to savor him. "Hands behind your head."

He swallowed hard, his green eyes glittering against the colorful Vegas backdrop. Still he did what she said. It surprised her, so she didn't waste any time. Moving down the length of his toned body, she worked his belt off and tugged his pants and boxer briefs down until they were at his knees. She didn't want to give him too much mobility. For a moment all she could do was stare at his cock. It curved up beautifully, thick and long. She knew exactly how it would feel inside her. Even thinking about him filling her made her ache, but right now wasn't about her. It was about him.

She slid off her jacket so that she was just in her heels now. Jay sucked in a breath. "Are you trying to torture me?"

The corner of her mouth turned up. "Maybe a little." She let her jacket drop next to them before shimmying back up his body until she hovered above him on all fours, her mouth right over his pulsing cock.

Looking up the length of his body, she smiled at the way he was completely tense, every single muscle pulled taut in anticipation. Leaning down, she flicked her tongue over the tip of his cock as she fisted it with one hand.

"Ellie," he groaned.

She took him fully in her mouth, not holding back as she teased and licked him. He shuddered under her stroking, saying her name like a prayer each time she took him as deep as she could. And he was still keeping his hands behind his head, something that surprised her immensely. His body started to shake and tremble the faster she worked him. Using her hands and mouth, she pleasured him until she knew he was close. The sounds he made turned her on more than she thought possible and she could feel her slickness against her inner thighs.

"I'm...wait, Ellie." Jay's strong hands landed on her shoulders, tugging her upward.

Pressing her hands against the cushion beneath them, she blinked, unsure why he was stopping her. She froze when she saw the raw need in his expression. Moving faster than she thought possible, he switched positions so that she was on her back. In a flurry of impossibly fast movements he stripped off the rest of his clothes.

Before she had a chance to enjoy the sight of all of him, of his deliciously muscular thighs, he grabbed her hips and roughly turned her over onto her stomach. It reminded her so much of their first time together that a shiver rolled down her spine. Her inner walls clenched again, desperate to be filled by him.

She'd meant this to be all about him tonight, but she should have known Jay would take over. Not that she was complaining.

His hand shook as he tugged her back to him, his cock pressing insistently between her thighs. But he didn't make a move to enter her, just slid his hard length along her slit until the head pushed against her clit. She jerked at the pleasurable sensation, her sensitive bundle of nerves tingling each time he stroked against her. He wasn't talking—he was past that point. When Jay got like this, there were no words between them. Just a raw, hot state of pleasure.

One of his big, callused hands slid down her spine, continuing until he smoothed his palm over the curve of her ass. He reached around and cupped her mound with his other. He pulled his hips back, sliding his erection back along her slickness as he began rubbing her clit. She loved the feel of skin on skin, of his body pressed to hers in the most intimate dance possible. How could she have ever thought she could leave this man? Even for his own protection? Jay was hers.

Back arching, she gasped and moved into his rhythm. He played her body perfectly, knowing exactly what she needed.

"Gonna come once I'm inside you, baby. Need...you to come first." His voice was as ragged as she'd ever heard it, telling her he was walking a razor's edge of control now.

"Inside me now." She knew it would push her over the edge. The only thing that would. Even the thought of him stretching her, pleasuring her, was making her wetter. And she couldn't find any more words than that. Just like him she was trembling, her body primed for him.

Not needing more than that, he thrust into her, his hardness filling her in one smooth stroke. Her back arched again as his fingers clasped around one of her hips. His other hand remained over her clit, his fingers teasing and stroking her as he continued to slam into her, all sense of control gone.

His movements were jerky, unsteady and each time he filled her he let out a ragged groan.

"I'm coming," she managed to rasp out, the only two words that would matter. She knew once she said them he'd let go of his own control. Which was exactly what she wanted.

He was barely hanging onto it and sure enough as soon as her own orgasm ricocheted through her in sharp, out-of-control waves, he grabbed both her hips, pumping into her as he shouted her name. She loved the feel of his fingers digging into her flesh, and hoped they'd leave a mark.

She lost all sense of time and her surroundings as he continued thrusting, releasing himself inside her in loud, unsteady shouts of pleasure until she finally collapsed against the lounge chair.

Or she would have if he hadn't caught her around the stomach with his big hand. Withdrawing from her, but holding her close, he nuzzled her neck as he dragged her upright, her back pressed against his muscular stomach.

"Sorry I didn't let you finish, I needed to come inside you," he murmured, his teeth grazing her ear.

She shivered, partially from the feel of his teeth and partially from the remnants of the climax still making her knees weak. "I'm surprised you let me get as far as I did."

"Next time, I promise."

She chuckled under her breath. "I'll believe it when I see it."

Taking her by surprise, he slid his hands up her ribs and only stopped when he cupped both her breasts. "And I can't believe I haven't paid any attention to these." He nipped her ear again as he slowly rolled her hard nipples between his fingers.

"Tonight…is supposed to be…about you." She struggled to get the words out as he continued pleasuring her. Already sensitive from the climax, his teasing felt even more intense.

"It's about both of us and we're just getting started." The dark edge to his voice sent a thrill down her spine, making her entire body tremble.

When she felt his cock start to harden against her back again she knew they were in for a long night. "I love you, Jay." She hadn't said the words since she'd attempted to run except for one heated conversation—and texting 'xo' didn't count. She needed him to know.

He froze for just a moment before kissing the side of her neck, raking his teeth and lips over her sensitive skin. "I love you too, baby. That's never been in question."

CHAPTER FIFTEEN

"You sure you're okay with everything?" Jay asked Ellie, pinning her with that intense stare as they sat in the back of the SUV.

She squirmed under his gaze. She'd called Kevin two minutes ago instead of texting him and told him where to meet her. She hated even hearing his voice, but it was unavoidable if she wanted to end this nightmare. They were at a small outside shopping center with two main exits and plenty of places for Jay's team to blend in and keep tabs on her. Just in case there was a problem, however, they'd tagged one of her shoes and her bracelet with a tracker.

She'd given Kevin as little time as possible to meet her so he couldn't bring in backup. And if he didn't show in fifteen minutes, she was leaving. Or that was what she'd told him. She'd wait an extra five because she wanted this over with. "Jeez, yes. Are you trying to freak me out?"

"Right," Iris murmured from the front passenger seat of the SUV. "You're supposed to be easing her fears."

"She's never done anything like this before, Iris," Jay snapped, his angry tone so out of character that Iris and

Hayden, who was in the driver's seat, both froze for a moment.

Finally Iris turned around to look at him. "You're right, and I'd be worried if this was Wyatt. But you've got to ease up. We've gone over this plan two dozen times."

Literally.

"And Ellie is smart. I've seen her handle those media vultures without breaking a sweat. She can do this."

Iris's words and her faith in Ellie were like a shock of adrenaline to her system. She could do this because it needed to be done. Because people she cared about were in danger. "I'm ready, Jay." Her statement dragged his gaze back around to her. "Now I have to go. I need to distance myself from you guys."

Jay nodded, his jaw tense before he dropped a fierce, demanding kiss on her lips that was a stark reminder of how he'd claimed her last night—multiple times. Then again this morning. Feeling a little dazed, she got out of the SUV, the slight tenderness between her legs another reminder of the night they'd shared. As soon as she stepped up onto the sidewalk, she heard the SUV's engine start. She knew they were just parking out of the way and that they'd have a visual on her the entire time, but she still couldn't help the nerves racing across her skin.

The only thing easing her fears was that this was a very public place and Kevin needed her alive. He wouldn't risk hurting her here or making a scene. She'd simply give him what he wanted, then they'd both go their separate ways. She'd leave in the rental car she'd gotten this morning, courtesy of her insurance company and if Kevin wanted to know how she'd lost her guards, she had an explanation ready.

Forcing herself not to look around too much, she went over the plan in her head. Wyatt and V were already in the shopping center near two different kiosks. They'd arrived an hour ago to get in place. They were both in disguise and had assured her she wouldn't recognize them. Wyatt would be drinking coffee and reading a paper and V would be drinking tea while working on a laptop. Roman and Logan were also there, pretending to be shoppers at two stores nearest the bench where she'd be waiting at. Hayden and Iris wouldn't be static though, they'd be moving around the entire time, staying close to the two exit areas. When Ellie left, she'd have one of them following her back to the casino.

Since Wyatt owned two of the businesses in this small shopping center—which was the reason they'd chosen it as a meeting place—Jay had access to the roof of one of the three-story buildings and was using his elevated position as a lookout. Completely hidden from view, he was keeping tabs on everything and everyone.

The entire team had earpieces provided by V and they were all staying in communication.

They wouldn't talk unless necessary since they wanted to keep the channel silent. Ellie was the only one who wouldn't have an earpiece but she did have a signal. If anything went wrong or she felt threatened, all she had to do was tug her hair out of the ponytail she'd pulled it into, and the team would act.

She walked to where five benches formed a circle around a fountain and sat at the one nearest the sunglasses kiosk. Just like she'd told Kevin. Not that he wouldn't recognize her. She certainly wasn't in disguise.

Directly across from her she saw a man with gray hair, a ball cap, jeans and a garish button-down flowered shirt reading a newspaper. A cup of coffee sat next to him on the bench. Was that Wyatt? She hoped so. Not wanting to stare, she glanced around, not for the rest of the team, but for signs of Kevin.

The minutes seemed to tick by slowly, endlessly, but after she looked at her cell phone she realized only five had passed. Taking a deep breath and steeling herself for this confrontation, she leaned back against the bench and tried to exude the attitude of someone in complete control. Of someone not afraid. Unfortunately, her quaking insides weren't listening to reason.

Jay didn't have to glance at his watch again to know that Murrell's time was almost up. If he didn't show, they were getting Ellie the hell out of here. He hated this plan even if it made the most sense. He also hated being so far away from her. But Iris and his brother had convinced him being the farthest away was the smartest place for him.

If he was in Wyatt or Vadim's position, he'd be too close to her and more likely to react if Kevin pulled anything. Which would blow her cover and ruin everything.

Jay had no doubt this asshole would try to see if Ellie had a backup team, if she was setting him up. It would be standard procedure for anyone with half a brain. Even though this guy was scum, he wasn't stupid. Jay had read up on his file early that morning before Ellie had woken up. The guy had gotten a bachelor's in engineering while in prison. It was a good degree and his grades had been decent enough. Either way it showed that he hadn't squandered his time. He'd also gotten out of prison far too early for his sentence. Which told Jay he'd likely snitched on someone higher up the food chain and cut a deal for a reduced sentence. That was just a guess since V hadn't been able to find out more.

"He's here," Iris said over their secure channel.

"Alone?" Jay immediately tensed, but didn't move from the shadows of his hiding spot. He'd chosen to use one of the four bell towers of the shopping center. Right now the sun was at his back so he'd have no distractions. From his angle he had a perfect visual of Ellie and the two exits. And the other three towers—which were just for show anyway—had been locked down so no one could gain access.

"No, Bejar's with him. Not sure if they brought more backup yet, but they're walking through the east side entrance. Doesn't look like they're carrying any weapons."

"I see them." Jay looked at the two men through binoculars, both casually dressed in jeans and plain, long-sleeved T-shirts. Nothing about them stood out. He couldn't see the outline of a weapon on either of them. Considering they'd just gotten out of prison, it was unlikely they'd be carrying anything. Too risky.

Without speaking to each other they split up, Bejar heading to one of the juice kiosks. He stood in line while Kevin looped around the entire place, not entering any stores. He just casually scanned people and the surroundings as he strolled. Yeah, he was looking to see if Ellie had backup.

Jay quickly glanced at Ellie. She was stiff against the bench, her gaze on Kevin as he loitered outside a shoe store. So she'd seen him. God, Jay hated that he couldn't be there with her. Even with just audible support.

"It's okay, baby," he murmured even though there was no way in hell she'd be able to hear him. After last night he was a hell of a lot more secure in what they had together. She'd made it clear she wasn't letting him go. He loved every second of how she'd shown him what he meant to her last night. And he wasn't letting her go either.

After a full loop of the place, Kevin made his way to the benches and sat two feet from Ellie. Her entire body went even more rigid. Neither of them looked at each other, but Jay could see Kevin saying something.

"I think it's just Bejar as his backup, but can't be sure," Iris murmured.

"You guys ready for this?" V asked before anyone could respond. "I wasn't sure if it would work so didn't say anything before."

Jay frowned, not sure what he was referring to when the sound of Ellie's voice came over the channel. Her words were tinny and distant, as if they were listening to a recording. V must have a recorder under the bench which explained the low quality.

"So you have what I need?" Murrell asked, his voice tight.

"Yes, but I need to know when you're planning...everything."

He snorted. "Why, so you can turn me in to the cops?"

"Are you stupid? I need to know so I have enough time to get out of town. Kevin, what you're planning is stupid. Why don't you just take your cash and forget this whole thing. You don't need this score. Christiansen will eventually figure out it was me who helped you." She sounded desperate, just like they'd planned.

Kevin scooted a foot closer, his hand landing on Ellie's shoulder. Ellie didn't push him away, but she looked annoyed. "And here I thought you might care about me, but you're just looking out for yourself."

"I'm looking out for *both* of us. You don't know what Christiansen is like. If he discovers you're involved he'll come after you hard. And he won't use the law to do it." Now she sounded terrified.

"What do you think De Luca will do to me if I back out? I don't have a choice at this point," he muttered.

Ellie jerked, her reaction so realistic it made Jay smile. "What the hell? You're working *with* De Luca?" she whispered the last part. "Are you insane?" Kevin hadn't told her about De Luca before so she had to appear truly shocked at this revelation.

Kevin watched her for a long moment before he scrubbed a hand over his face. Shrugging, he looked away from her, glancing around the center. People milled around the kiosks and in and out of the stores. It wasn't too busy, but steady enough and with plenty of people for Jay's team to blend in. When Kevin seemed satisfied he turned back to Ellie. "He doesn't know anything about before. And I didn't originally plan to work with him. It just happened that way."

"How?" Ellie demanded.

"I might have been bragging to someone in his crew about how I knew you and that if I wanted I could get my hands on...the collection. With your help." His inference to the jewels was understood, but he wasn't coming out and being specific. It was clear he trusted Ellie enough, obviously because he thought she was alone. And it also stood to reason that he didn't have backup listening since he'd brought up the subject of De Luca to her.

Ellie cursed and turned away from him, as if disgusted. "That's so stupid. Now you're dragging me down with you. And all because of your big mouth. Why am I not surprised?"

"If I remember right, you used to like my mouth." The softly spoken innuendo made Jay's blood turn icy.

Turning away from the sight of them, he continued scanning the area while listening to their conversation. Bejar had taken up a spot on a bench directly across from them on the other side of the fountain. He was too far away to hear anything but close enough that Jay didn't like it. "Anyone see anything else?" Jay asked the team. *Focus.* He had to stay focused on the mission, not that bastard's words to Ellie.

As everyone murmured negative responses, Ellie made a disgusted sound to Murrell. "I was seventeen and stupid."

"So what, you think you're too good for me now?"

"Are you kidding me? I thought you wanted information, not to dredge up the past. Your big mouth got us into this mess and I'm walking away. I don't have time for this." Ellie stood, her willingness to walk from him a solidification of her cover.

Kevin reached out and grabbed her forearm. On instinct Jay reached for his SIG. Not like he could do anything with it from here. Another smart reason why he'd been relegated to the bell tower. If he'd been close, Jay might not have been able to stop himself from making a move. It didn't matter that he'd had the best training in the world. Seeing another male's hand on Ellie like that made all his training and control dissipate.

Ellie didn't yank away, but sat back down, her body rigid. "Get your hand off me or I'll rip your nuts off."

The threat was so un-Ellie like it made Jay smile. Hell yeah, that was his woman.

Murrell released her, but moved in close. Too close. "You give me what I want and my money and we're even."

"I'll give you the plans you need, but that's it. It was damn hard getting these. If you take this file, then I'm out. I'm taking that money and starting over somewhere. If you let this drop I'll give you the cash and you can leave town. If not, I'm not sticking around waiting for Christiansen to take me out."

"Your boss is really like that?"

Ellie snorted indelicately, as if Murrell was stupid. "He didn't get to be so wealthy playing by the rules, and he's a former Marine. What do you think?"

That was actually true, Jay knew. Not the part about him killing people, but Wyatt definitely didn't play by the rules.

"I think I want that file *and* my money," Murrell growled low in his throat, his words barely audible on the scratchy audio feed.

"You get one or the other. You choose," Ellie said, all confidence but Jay knew this was hard on her.

When Murrell paused, Jay could actually feel the tension from the rest of the team members as they waited for his response. They were all ready to strike at Murrell if he made one wrong move. Not that it did anything to ease the clawing, aching fear he experienced every second the woman he loved was sitting next to that piece of garbage.

Finally Murrell sighed. "How'd you get this information anyway? And how do I know it's good?"

"You'll know as soon as you look at it and it's none of your business how I got it."

"How?" There was a warning note in Murrell's voice that made all the hair on Jay's neck stand on end. What he wouldn't give to end the guy's life right now.

"I have full access to my boss's computer. I found some backup files on there. And it wasn't easy to access. I covered my tracks, but he'll eventually figure out it was me who leaked them. I...also included some other information for you. It should help if you decide to do this asinine thing. Now what's your choice?"

He paused again, but this time the silence was much shorter. "The file. And if you double cross me, I'll kill that pussy you're living with and make you watch."

Ellie laughed, mocking Murrell. "You're an idiot," she said, seemingly unfazed. But Jay recognized the underlying thread of emotion she was trying desperately to hide. Fear. For him. Throat tight, he looked away and did another scan of the perimeter and exits as they continued to talk.

"So what's his deal, anyway?" The question sounded casual, but Jay watched the subtle way Murrell tensed, turning his legs and body toward Ellie. He wanted the answer to this question, the nuances of his body language giving him away.

She reached into her jeans' pocket and smoothly slid the flash drive into Murrell's palm as if they were simply shaking hands. "I'm not talking about my personal life. This is it. You do whatever you want with it, I'm not helping you anymore. Now that I know you're working with De Luca I know you won't tell him about that money. And it's mine now. I'm taking it and leaving since you chose the stupid option."

Murrell grabbed Ellie's jaw in a tight grip. "You've got a fiery little mouth on you now, bitch."

Jay headed for the exit, ready to race down the stairs, but froze at Iris's words. "Stay put, Jay. She's okay."

Before he could respond, Murrell made a gasping, choking sound. Then he heard Ellie's voice, loud and clear. "I told you not to touch me again."

"Your girl just grabbed his junk and twisted," Roman said under his breath, awe in his voice.

Relief slammed through Jay with the intensity of a fifty cal. He resumed his post, using the shadows to cover him as he moved back to the opening. As he slid back into place Jay saw Murrell limping away in the same direction he'd come. Bejar left his seat at the same time, going with Murrell, not in Ellie's direction. Lucky for him.

"I've got eyes on him. I'll tail him until he leaves the parking lot," Iris said.

"V and I are shadowing Ellie until she gets to her car," Wyatt said quietly and Jay watched as he stood from the nearby bench, moving ahead of Ellie.

It still stunned Jay that his boss had managed to disguise himself as an old man so well. Even though nothing would completely relieve Jay until Ellie was back in their hotel suite and in his arms again, some of his tension fled as he watched her head to her rental car, Wyatt and V nearby in case anything happened. They'd have to blow their cover to protect her, but that was a risk they were all willing to take.

Now that the first part of their plan had been put into motion, they just had to wait for Murrell and De Luca to make their move. Unfortunately they couldn't pinpoint exactly when they'd strike so they'd have to be on guard 24/7 until De Luca and Kevin were completely out of the picture. Until that happened, Jay knew he'd never relax again.

CHAPTER SIXTEEN

"What the hell was that all about?" Tadeo asked the second they shut the doors to the minivan.

Still seething, Kevin unclenched his jaw, struggling to take a breath. He couldn't believe Ellie had grabbed his junk like that. She was nothing like the quiet, docile girl he remembered. He shifted against the passenger seat, trying to get more comfortable, his balls protesting in pain as he moved. Stupid bitch. "Needed to remind her who was in charge."

"How'd that work for you, *mano*?" Tadeo rolled his eyes as he steered out of the parking lot.

Kevin didn't bother responding as he turned in his seat to see if they were being followed. He doubted it since no one had made themselves known when he'd grabbed Ellie's jaw. And she hadn't been looking around for backup. No, she'd just gone straight for his goods. "You see anyone out of place back there?"

"Don't think so. Besides, when you manhandled her like that we'd have known if she had backup."

"Yeah." It was partially why he'd grabbed her like that, but mainly he'd wanted to wipe that obnoxious look off her pretty face. He couldn't believe the way she'd talked to him. If they hadn't been in public he'd have done a lot more than grab her. Taking his aggression out on this new version of her could be very therapeutic.

Tadeo shook his head, chuckling as he continued. "Can't believe she grabbed you like that. It was crazy. You shoulda seen your face. You at least get you what we need?"

Kevin wanted to knock that stupid smile off Tadeo's face, but he kept his cool. Until he had his own crew to back him up, Tadeo was one of his few allies in Vegas. He could let a little disrespect slide, especially since he knew Tadeo wasn't being malicious. "Let's find out," he said, pulling out the stolen laptop he'd brought from under his seat. His balls still hurt, but the pain was already fading.

Flipping it open, he waited for it to boot up before plugging the flash drive in. In case she'd decided to plant a tracking device in it, he copied all the files. Soon he'd destroy the flash drive and toss the remaining pieces.

As file after file popped up, his heart rate increased and his anger began to fade. She might be a bitch now but it looked as if she'd come through. He quickly scanned the standard building plans, then the additional plans that showed all the security measures Christiansen had put into place. The information on the extra security was gold. He'd have to go over everything more in depth once they had more privacy but at first glance he knew exactly how to steal the jewels.

Continuing through the rest of the files, he paid special attention to the security schedule she'd given him. And that was how he knew she wasn't lying. He didn't have all the guards' routines yet, but the ones he did have matched perfectly with her information. If she'd lied it would have made him more suspicious.

Looked like this was going to work out in his favor. He might have made a mistake by running his mouth in front of one of Tadeo's cousins—who had then relayed everything to De Luca—about being able to rob Christiansen, but everything was going to work out. That was what happened when you thought big.

Eventually he'd take over De Luca's territory, but for now he'd create a name for himself with this robbery. He'd become known in certain circles and it would give him the credentials he needed to start his own crew. And Ellie was definitely going to die after the heist.

He hadn't been sure before, but now he didn't care what De Luca did to her, especially after the way she'd disrespected him. He still wanted his money too, but if he had to give it up for this information, it would be worth it in the long run.

CHAPTER SEVENTEEN

Three days later

Jay stared at the monitor in V's office, unable to believe De Luca had sent Kevin and his crew in to steal the Dragon Collection only three days after receiving the plans from Ellie. "They're actually good," Jay murmured, watching as the small four man team worked together in perfect synchronicity.

"Laziness or incompetency was never his problem," Ellie said. "He just thinks the world owes him and likes to take from those he views as having the success he should have."

Jay tightened his arm around her waist, pulling her close. "After tonight he's never going to bother you again."

Sitting on one of the chairs in V's office, Ellie was in Jay's lap, right where she belonged. It was just after midnight and they'd received a call from Wyatt that everything was going down tonight. One of the security teams he'd had stationed around the perimeter of the hotel had spotted Murrell. Then V had verified him with their facial recognition software. Just once, because

Murrell and his small crew had been very careful about avoiding security cameras. It was pretty damn impossible considering how many they had at the Serafina, but he'd come close.

As they continued watching, the office door made a soft whooshing sound as it opened behind them. Wyatt stepped into the office with a satisfied grin on his face. Even with the late hour the man was dressed in a three-piece custom-made suit looking every bit the billionaire he was. "Everything's in place. Hurley's inside man came through. SWAT now has the location of the meeting place after they take the jewels. Apparently De Luca plans to eliminate Murrell at the meeting. No loose ends. It won't get that far though."

"That's too bad," Jay muttered, earning a half-grin from Wyatt.

"The team will infiltrate the moment the jewels are in De Luca's hands. Murrell is going down too and I've been assured there's no chance of him getting out early again. Not after this. We're handing the cops De Luca and the state's attorney is feeling very generous about that."

Ellie let out a big sigh, melting against Jay. "I can't believe this is almost over. Thank you guys. All of you. So much. Words will never be enough, but…" Her voice cracked once but she continued. "Just thank you."

Wyatt's expression softened a fraction as he nodded. "Something else that might make you feel even better. That bastard Leonard is going away for a long time too."

At that both Jay and Ellie straightened. "For what?" Ellie asked before he could.

"Involvement in drug trafficking and the skin trade. It's why Hurley was there undercover. Your appearance that day moved his time table up when Leonard fired him, but it worked out for the best. Been waiting to tell you guys, but couldn't until the charges were official," he said before stepping over to the monitors and murmuring quietly to Vadim.

Ellie shifted against Jay's lap, her dark eyes bright with something he recognized. Hope. "If they don't need us here anymore there's something I want to do. I know it's late, but—"

Unable to stop himself, Jay brushed a kiss over her soft lips. "Let's do it," he murmured.

Her eyebrows pulled together. "You don't even know what it is."

"I think I can guess." She wanted to retrieve the money Murrell had stolen. She still hadn't told him where it was, but Jay knew her better than anyone.

"I don't want to keep any of it. If we turn it in, the cops will just keep it as evidence. We should donate it."

He grinned. "I can think of a few places that could use it."

"Me too. We'll need to change...and get shovels."

"I'm going to pretend I don't know what you two are talking about," Wyatt said without turning from the monitors. "I'll text you once they've cleared the hotel and you're good to go. Use one of the employee exits and take what you need from maintenance."

Kevin's heart was an erratic beat in his ears as he and Tadeo slid into the backseat of the nondescript SUV they'd used for this heist. He couldn't believe how smoothly everything had gone. Everything Ellie had given him was perfect. Which should have eased the tension that had settled in his gut.

Instead it was worse.

The lead ball of worry in his chest that had been with him the past three days was jagged and angry, telling him something was wrong. He just couldn't figure out what it was. De Luca had told him and Tadeo that the rumor was Ellie had split town. No one had seen her since the meeting at the shopping center and while it hadn't been officially announced, she hadn't been seen with Christiansen publicly. Her boyfriend had been with the billionaire, but not Ellie. De Luca was pissed, thinking that Kevin had told her to run, but Tadeo had assured the man that Kevin hadn't. That she'd run because she'd known what would happen to her.

Guess she hadn't been kidding about leaving town. De Luca would catch up to her eventually. Or maybe Christiansen. Kevin didn't care as long as she ended up dead.

The bright neon lights of the city flew by as they cruised down the main strip. Even when they turned off onto a side street, the colorful display didn't fade. This place truly never slept. Right now he felt as if he'd never sleep again either. He was always like this after a job. While this one had gone smoothly, it was still an adrenaline rush, stealing something so valuable. Something no one had attempted before. It hadn't been easy either, but with the right plans and all the practice they'd done, the job had gone off without a hitch.

The driver was talking quietly to someone on his earpiece—one of De Luca's men or De Luca himself—and the man in the passenger seat wasn't paying attention to them when Tadeo slid something over to Kevin. His friend didn't look at him as he handed it over, but continued staring out his window.

As that ball in his stomach expanded into a full-fledged adrenaline dump, he casually cupped the piece of paper in his right palm, keeping it low against his outer thigh as he read it.

Don't react. De Luca's getting busted tonight. You're supposed to be there too, but I can't do that to you. No other time to warn you. Jump out at next stop and run. Don't stay in city, cops will find you. Sorry, mano.

Kevin felt all the blood drain from his face, his fingers turning numb in his gloves. He didn't dare look at Tadeo. This wasn't a joke. His friend wouldn't mess with him about this. For a split second he wondered if this was some bullshit way to cut him out of the eventual sale of the Dragon Collection, but knew that didn't make sense. De Luca would have other ways to get rid of him. Something he'd thought long and hard about. In the end, there had been more reasons for De Luca to keep him alive in the long run, especially since Kevin had proven himself to be a valuable asset.

So this letter was real. And if Tadeo knew his boss was getting busted it meant he'd been somehow involved in it. He must be working with the cops, which explained why he hadn't been able to tell him before now. They'd been at De Luca's place the last three days preparing for this job. The man hadn't been willing to let any of them out of his sight for even a moment. Tadeo was taking a huge risk by doing this, by letting him go.

A small thread of guilt wormed its way through him because Kevin wasn't sure he'd have done the same thing for Tadeo. No, he knew he wouldn't have.

As they neared a traffic light that had just turned red, he slowly reached out and slid the lock to unlock. Knowing there was no time to second guess himself, he jerked the door open and jumped from the slow rolling vehicle. There were shouts of alarm from behind him and one car honked, but he ignored everything as his feet hit the sidewalk. Racing back in the opposite direction the SUV was headed, he didn't turn around. Unless they planned to open fire on him, they'd never catch him. And there was no way they'd risk engaging him in a chase or shootout, not when they were carrying those diamonds.

Once he reached the upcoming corner, he risked a glance behind him and didn't see the SUV anymore. He knew he couldn't stick around here long. Not if Tadeo's note was real. No, he'd need to steal a car and head out of the city limits. And he knew just the place to go.

Ellie had taken him to a cluster of caves out in the desert once. He'd been there twice since he'd gotten out of prison. It had been clear no one had been there in a long time so he'd used it to stash a run bag. Because he believed in always being prepared. Especially after going to prison. There was no way in hell he was going back. Originally he'd scoped out the caves to see if she'd hidden his money there but he hadn't found anything. No disturbed earth and no tracks other than from a few coyotes. Hell, he hadn't even been sure she'd kept his money, but he'd had to look before he contacted her.

Now he was grateful for his hideout. He could stay there for a few days and wait out a manhunt if the cops gave chase. Since he couldn't ask Tadeo for more details he had no clue if the police would care enough about him to lock down roads or not. He couldn't take the chance they would and get caught at a roadblock.

CHAPTER EIGHTEEN

"It's impressive how well you hid all this," Jay said to her as he looked down at the dust covered bags of cash on the cave floor.

Ellie shrugged, holding onto the handle of the shovel as she half-leaned against it. A light coating of dust clung to them after the twenty minute trek to the cave from where they'd parked, more after the actual digging. "The small rocks hid the disturbed earth well in case any hikers stumbled onto these caves."

Jay grunted. "Doubtful, considering how far out of the way this place is."

"I know, but still. Plus, Kevin knew about this place." At her words, Jay stilled. The light from the battery-operated lanterns played across his hard features, but it was hard to read him.

"Should I not talk about him?" she asked. Ever since she'd met up with Kevin at the shopping center Jay had been uber-protective. But he hadn't spoken about Kevin directly since then. It had all been in terms of 'the plan' and how they planned to make sure he went back to jail. She'd basically been on lockdown with no contact with anyone at work since then. Jay and Wyatt had wanted to make it appear as if she'd left town. They'd been vague when questioned about her by hotel employees and even though she'd been going stir crazy in the suite, she'd understood the need for her to remain out of sight.

Shoulders relaxing, Jay shook his head as he let out a long breath. "You can talk about your past. I don't ever want you to hide any part of yourself from me. I just hate that guy for bringing so much crap into your life."

She smiled, understanding. "I get it. And it's not—"

When Jay suddenly froze, his huge body going impossibly still, a streak of fear raced up her spine. She hadn't heard anything. He held a finger up to his mouth and immediately turned off the nearest lantern with a quick flip of a switch. As the cave plunged into semi-darkness, he pulled a gun from his ankle holster. Bending down, she started to turn off the other lantern on the ground next to the biggest bag of cash when a familiar, hated voice echoed through the cave.

"Drop the gun or I shoot the bitch," Kevin said, his voice low and angry.

Ellie's head snapped up, fear lancing through her as she scanned the mouth of the cave. With the light next to her face and the front of the cave so dark it was impossible to see much except the silhouette of Kevin's body.

Jay stood about three feet away from her and a couple feet closer to the mouth of the cave. She watched as his hand clenched once around his gun. It was angled down as he hadn't fully stood. By the time he raised it, Kevin would have already shot one of them. She knew he'd shoot her first. She also knew that if Jay dropped his weapon, Kevin would kill them both. While she had no clue why he was here, he was, and that told her he knew she'd lied to him. Her heart stuttered in her chest.

"Don't drop it," she said, her voice strong.

Jay still hadn't moved as Kevin stepped deeper into the cave with them. Now she got a good view of him. Like an angry rain cloud, his expression was as dark as the black clothes he was still wearing from the casino robbery.

"You might hit me, but I'll blow her head off before you raise it." Kevin's voice was calm as he held a gun pointed directly at her. He wouldn't miss either. Not with this big freaking spotlight illuminating her face.

She still hadn't stood from her crouched position, too terrified to make any sudden movements and have him get trigger happy.

The silence in the cave seemed like a giant void until Jay finally spoke, his voice low and calm. "I'm dropping it now," he said as he placed his gun on the hard earth.

Even with all his training, Ellie realized he was too far away to attempt rushing Kevin. Kevin would shoot him before he'd made it two, maybe three steps. She could actually see it unfolding in her mind and fought the nausea swelling inside her.

"What are you doing here?" she rasped out.

Kevin trained his gun on Jay as he stood up, making Ellie's panic skyrocket to epic proportions. He couldn't shoot Jay, he just couldn't. She refused to believe it would happen even though she saw the menacing glint in her ex's eyes.

"I'm still not sure," he said to Ellie, but kept his gaze and gun trained on Jay.

All Ellie could seem to focus on was that gun, her tunnel vision threatening to make her lose the small window of opportunity she might have. Mentally shaking herself, she looked at Kevin's face, tried to keep her voice steady. "What do you mean?"

"I mean exactly what I said, I'm not fucking sure," he snapped. "After the heist one of my boys told me to run because a big bust was going down on De Luca. Something tells me you two know something about that. Was the whole heist a setup? Are the jewels even real?"

"It wasn't a setup," Jay said smoothly, drawing Kevin's attention from Ellie. "But I think your friend lied to you."

No! Ellie wanted to shout, but understood what Jay was doing, understood that she'd get only one chance to save them. From her crouched position, she reached back with her right hand and wrapped her fingers around the revolver tucked into the back of her pants. Jay had given it to her for this desert trek. It had been in case they ran into wild animals and needed to scare them off.

Not to defend themselves from a real life monster. Unfortunately that's what she had to do.

"No way he lied," Kevin continued, shaking his head vehemently. His hand shook as he punctuated each angry word. And all his attention was on Jay.

On the man she loved.

Overcome by the strangest calm, Ellie used his distraction to her advantage and brought the weapon around. Since it was a double action revolver she didn't have to pull the hammer back.

She simply fired and kept firing until she'd emptied the chamber. Kevin dropped where he stood, his hands flailing out as she nailed him in the stomach then the chest. The cave echoed loudly from the report, her ears ringing and her hands trembling as she stared at Kevin's fallen form.

When he didn't move from the dusty ground, she dropped her arm, but couldn't stop the shaking that had taken over her entire body. She'd been to the shooting range with Jay multiple times and knew how to use guns. Hell, she lived near the desert, practically everyone here owned a gun. But she'd never thought to use it on a person before. Not unless absolutely necessary.

She could hear Kevin struggling for breath, the ragged sounds permeating the cave until they simply stopped, but she couldn't force herself to walk any closer to him. Her feet refused to listen to her brain.

Jay moved to Kevin's body and kicked his gun out of the way before bending down next to him. He stayed there for a long moment, searching for a pulse beneath his jaw before standing and turning back to her. "He's gone," he murmured.

Ellie opened her mouth to respond, but couldn't make her voice work. Jay moved toward her cautiously, as if she was a frightened animal. "You're okay, baby," he murmured soothingly.

She blinked once, everything coming back into focus in a rush. Placing the revolver on the ground she nodded and finally found her voice again. "I know. I...he was going to kill both of us."

Jay nodded, his expression fierce as he gathered her into his arms. She gripped him tight, linking her arms around his waist and burying her face in his chest. Tears burned her eyes, not because of Kevin but because she could have lost Jay. A sob built in her throat but she bit it back and held onto Jay, soaking up his strength. She wasn't sure how long they stood there holding each other but eventually Jay pulled back.

He swiped a callused thumb over her cheek, his expression gentle but determined. "We've got to make a decision here and now. Call the cops and explain the money or leave with the money and never tell a soul about this. No one. I won't even tell Hayden about this. Just you and me and the desert will know. Before you decide make sure it's something you can live with. I say we leave this piece of garbage to the coyotes, but it's not my call."

She wasn't sure what it said about her, but she didn't have to think long about her decision. That money could do a hell of a lot of good in the right hands but if the police were called it would end up in a dusty locker somewhere. Worse than that, if they got involved, it would drag Jay deeper into this mess. How could he explain why he was out here in the desert with her digging up money? And how the hell would she even explain the money in the first place? She couldn't do that to Jay. She'd acted to defend him and could live with what she'd done, knowing there had been no other choice. Since Kevin didn't have any family she wouldn't be stealing closure from anyone if he just disappeared. "We leave and tell no one."

Relief flooded his expression. Nodding, Jay stepped back from her. He lifted one of the smaller bags of cash and handed it to her. "Take this to the car and wait there. I'll be back once I've taken care of his body and I'll bring the rest of the money."

Frowning, she shook her head and dropped the bag before picking up the nearest shovel. "We do this together." Because there was no way in hell she was making him deal with this all on his own, not when it was her fault he'd been dragged into this mess in the first place.

She knew she could trust Jay with this secret forever. Just as he was showing that he clearly trusted her.

CHAPTER NINETEEN

Ellie waited as her computer shut down before pushing back from her desk. Even though it was Sunday, she'd decided to come in and get some work done. Mainly that had involved answering the hundreds of emails she'd received for those few days where she'd just disappeared. After they were sure that De Luca and his crew were under arrest and the charges were sticking, Wyatt had told everyone she'd been sick with a terrible flu. So now she had a bunch of flowers and balloons lining her office.

Which made her smile.

She really did love working here. But more than anything she loved Jay. So much that it filled her until she wanted to tell everyone how wonderful the feeling was. Which she knew was stupid. But now that he knew about her past and didn't judge her, all that fear she'd had before was just gone. He loved her for exactly who she was. After everything they'd been through together she knew without a doubt that Jay was the kind of man to be there for her through the good times and the tough ones. Just as she would be there for him. Always.

He'd wanted her to work from home today but she'd known exactly how that would have gone. She wouldn't have gotten a single thing done.

As she grabbed her purse, her office door opened, surprising her. This floor was private to her, Wyatt and the security staff, and she knew Wyatt had taken the night off to spend it with Iris. Since the security personnel rarely needed her, she was surprised when Vadim stepped inside. She'd thought he would know their boss was off for the evening. "Hey, V, Wyatt's not here."

"I know, I came to see you." His voice was soft, non-threatening and still, the man made her nervous.

"Okay." She stayed where she was, purse in hand.

As if sensing her hesitancy, he half-smiled and took a step back toward the door, putting more distance between them in a clear attempt to put her more at ease. "I saw on the news that Santa Claus visited Vegas early Thursday morning."

Ellie knew what he was referring to but wasn't sure why he was bringing it up. Iris, Wyatt, and Hayden must have guessed what she and Jay had done—anonymously donating the money to various non-profit organizations, not the other thing—but no one had said a word because nothing needed to be said. "Yeah, me too."

V stood there for a long moment as if trying to find the right words and she wondered if some of her anxiety around him had more to do with his lack of social skills than anything else. Finally he cleared his throat, almost nervously. "It was good what you did..." He trailed off in that odd way of his, shrugging.

She still thought he was a bit intimidating, but she smiled and stepped out from her desk. "I'm heading out. Want to walk me to the elevators?"

Smiling, sort of, he nodded and opened the door, stepping out before her. Now she realized he definitely wanted to put her at ease and this must be his way of showing it. Limited social skills she could deal with, especially since he'd gone above and beyond to help her. Sure it had been at Wyatt's asking, but he still hadn't had to do it.

"So the real jewels are back in place?" she asked, making small talk.

"Yeah, oversaw them being moved from the vault to the display myself. Security's even tighter now. They won't be here much longer anyway. The museum is taking them back." He was hard to read, but sounded pleased about that.

"I bet De Luca was pissed to find out the jewels he got were fake." To know that his own man had betrayed him.

V just grunted a sound of agreement.

Tadeo Bejar was testifying against De Luca for not only being the mastermind of the jewel heist but for a whole mess of other things including drug and human trafficking. He hadn't admitted to tipping Kevin off, but the cops were pretty certain that was why Kevin had run the way he had. No one could prove it though and since Bejar wasn't a threat to her, Ellie didn't really care. Kevin wasn't going to be a threat to anyone ever again. The cops were still looking for him and she felt bad about that since they'd never find a body, but there was nothing to be done. The police assumed he'd gone on the run and would attempt to escape to Mexico and that assumption was fine with her.

After saying goodbye to Vadim she got into the elevator and pressed L for lobby. She'd left her rental car with valet earlier because the thought of walking to and from the parking garage alone had made her nervous. She knew Kevin couldn't hurt her, but after what had happened in the desert, she still felt raw and vulnerable and yeah, scared. Being back at home with Jay eased most of her lingering fears, but she wasn't naïve enough to think they'd go away overnight.

It belatedly registered that the elevator had gone up instead of down. Frowning, she pressed the L button again but the doors opened on one of the top floors and stayed there. She depressed the button a couple more times but nothing happened. "What the heck?" she muttered to herself. She'd have to call maintenance or take another elevator because she wasn't walking down a bazillion flights of stairs in her heels.

Stepping out into the tiled area, she paused at the sight of a big white sign with a red arrow drawn onto it. Underneath it said 'This way, Ellie'. Her heart skipped a beat at the sight, a slight smile tugging at her lips.

Was this Jay's doing? It had to be. She headed in the direction of the arrow toward the entrance of one of the hotel's viewing floors. After she walked through the open glass doors, she immediately spotted a small round table with candles, a bottle of champagne chilling on ice and two chairs set right next to one of the ceiling-to-floor length windows. This floor was for tourists to be able to view the entire city, but it was closed after a certain time.

"Jay?" she called out, stepping farther into the expansive, open room, butterflies dancing in her stomach.

Music filtered over the hidden speakers and it took her a moment to realize it was the first song they'd ever made love to. Not from the first time they'd been together, because there had been no music then, but she remembered this playing one hot evening when Jay had gotten frisky and they hadn't gone directly home after work. Instead they'd been a little adventurous in his truck in the private parking garage. And this song had been playing. How had he even remembered that? And where was he?

She slowly strode toward the table, the bright lights of the city glittering in every direction she looked. Sometimes the hotel catered events up here and the only place where he could be was the small kitchen galley in the middle of the room. She wasn't sure if she was supposed to find him or… Jay strode out one of the swinging galley doors a moment later, his expression intense.

"Hey," she managed to rasp out.

"Hey, yourself." He swallowed hard as he approached, almost faltering. It was so out of character, she wasn't sure what to make of it.

"What is all this?" she asked, her voice shaking. She thought she might know, but didn't want to hope.

His green eyes flashed against the outside lights as he stopped in front of her. For a moment it appeared as if he would reach for her hips in that all too familiar way of his, but instead, he went down on one knee—and her own just about buckled. Clearing his throat, he held up a small blue box and flipped it open to reveal a sparkly solitaire emerald-cut diamond. "After everything we've been through together, I hope you know by now that there will never be anyone else for me. Marry me, Ellie."

His intensely spoken words shattered through her. She nodded, struggling to find her voice as tears clogged her throat.

As she reached for the box, he shook his head. "Say the word."

"Yes. Yes, yes, yes!" Her answer came out raspy and unsteady and she was thankful when he slid the ring onto her left hand ring finger. It was a perfect fit.

Tears blurring her vision, she fell to her knees in front of him, wrapping her arms around his neck. His own grip on her hips was tight and possessive. "You're so sneaky, setting all this up. You got security to override me and send the elevator up here?"

Smiling smugly, he brushed his lips over hers tenderly, but she could feel the underlying strength and need humming through him. He nodded as he answered. "Yeah. I thought you'd be done hours ago so I finally sent Vadim to check on you."

Leaning into Jay, she kissed him again, this time harder, her lips melding to his, their tongues dancing in an erotic rhythm that made her entire body flare to life. When he finally pulled back, she was breathless. "I love you," she murmured, wondering what she'd done to deserve this wonderful man, but not questioning it any longer. She wouldn't live in fear that it might be taken away just because she allowed herself to be happy. Because she wouldn't let it. Jay was a man worth fighting her demons and insecurities for.

"I love you too." When he tugged her back into another toe-curling kiss she hoped this floor was empty because she planned to strip him completely naked and kiss every inch of his delicious body.

Starting tonight she planned to put all the darkness behind her and start a bright, new life with the man she loved by her side.

ACKNOWLEDGMENTS

Thank you so much to Kari Walker and Carolyn Crane for reading early versions of this book and giving valuable insight. I also owe a huge thanks to Joan Turner for proofreading. For my readers, as always, thank you for not only reading my stories but for also spreading the word about them! Every day I'm so grateful for your support. I'm also incredibly thankful for the beautiful design work by Jaycee with Sweet 'N Spicy Designs. Another thank you to my fabulous assistant, Tanya Hyatt, who does so many behind the scenes things so I can focus on writing. Last, but never least, I'm thankful to God for so many wonderful opportunities.

COMPLETE BOOKLIST

Red Stone Security Series
No One to Trust
Danger Next Door
Fatal Deception
Miami, Mistletoe & Murder
His to Protect
Breaking Her Rules
Protecting His Witness
Sinful Seduction

The Serafina: Sin City Series
First Surrender
Sensual Surrender
Sweetest Surrender

Deadly Ops Series
Targeted
Bound to Danger (2014)

Non-series Romantic Suspense
Running From the Past
Everything to Lose
Dangerous Deception

Dangerous Secrets
Killer Secrets
Deadly Obsession
Danger in Paradise
His Secret Past

Paranormal Romance
Destined Mate
Protector's Mate
A Jaguar's Kiss
Tempting the Jaguar
Enemy Mine
Heart of the Jaguar

Moon Shifter Series
Alpha Instinct
Lover's Instinct (novella)
Primal Possession
Mating Instinct
His Untamed Desire (novella)
Avenger's Heat

Darkness Series
Darkness Awakened
Taste of Darkness (2014)

ABOUT THE AUTHOR

Katie Reus is the *New York Times* and *USA Today* bestselling author of the Red Stone Security series, the Moon Shifter series and the Deadly Ops series. She fell in love with romance at a young age thanks to books she pilfered from her mom's stash. Years later she loves reading romance almost as much as she loves writing it.

However, she didn't always know she wanted to be a writer. After changing majors many times, she finally graduated summa cum laude with a degree in psychology. Not long after that she discovered a new love. Writing. She now spends her days writing dark paranormal romance and sexy romantic suspense. For more information on Katie please visit her website: www.katiereus.com. Also find her on twitter @katiereus or visit her on facebook at: www.facebook.com/katiereusauthor.

Made in the USA
Lexington, KY
28 October 2016